The tears were so close to the surface, and I was feeling so dizzy, so rotten, that talking about it now was the last thing I wanted to do. But they had the right to know. So I began by admitting my error. "I hitched. *We* hitched, from Santa Monica. . . . I know," I said. "You warned me not to. I promised I wouldn't. But I did." My mother put a hand over her mouth, to hide— what? At the time I thought it was pity. Now I wonder if it wasn't anger.

"It was stupid," I went on. "Oh, God, it was stupid! You told me at least a hundred times. If only I'd listened!"

GLORIA D. MIKLOWITZ has written more than twenty books for young readers. Currently, she teaches creative writing at Pasadena City College. She and her husband live near Pasadena, California.

Did You Hear What Happened to Andrea?

Gloria D. Miklowitz

LAUREL-LEAF BOOKS bring together under a single imprint outstanding works of fiction and nonfiction particularly suitable for young adult readers, both in and out of the classroom. Charles F. Reasoner, Professor of Elementary Education, New York University, is consultant to this series.

Published by
Dell Publishing Co., Inc.
1 Dag Hammarskjold Plaza
New York, New York 10017

For J., my husband and best friend

For information address
Delacorte Press, New York, New York.
Laurel-Leaf Library ® TM 766734,
Dell Publishing Co., Inc.

ISBN: 0-440-91853-7
RL: 5.7

Reprinted by arrangement with Delacorte Press
Printed in the United States of America
First Laurel-Leaf printing—July 1981
Fourth Laurel-Leaf printing—November 1981

Many people deserve thanks and appreciation for their help in the writing of this book—especially those I worked with and learned from on the Pasadena Rape Hotline; Nancy and Kim, rape victims, who generously shared their feelings and insights with me; the Pasadena Vice Squad, particularly Officer Denis, who explained police procedures; Helen Jones, friend and critic, and my writing peers who lived through each chapter with me; and finally my really fine editors at Delacorte—Alice Bregman and Judy Gitenstein, whose creative criticism and encouragement helped make Andrea a better book than it might have been.

1

I remember everything about that day, from the minute I woke up, till it happened.

As soon as I opened my eyes, I knew it was going to be hot and smoggy. That's how it is in Los Angeles in August. In June, it's still foggy and cool. Then suddenly, just after school lets out, the heat and smog set in until September. The only thing to do then is stay where it's air-conditioned, or else go to the beach.

Outside, the Browns' rainbird was chuk-chukking its way across their back lawn. Nearer still, next to my bedroom window, the doves were cooing their comforting, safe sounds high up in the elm tree. From the kitchen I heard muffled voices, probably the radio, because from nine o'clock on, my mother tunes into Michael Jackson's talk show and carries him around the house.

Someone had fried bacon. I could smell it and it made my mouth water. It was probably for my older sister, Sue. She's on a new diet. Dr. Stillman's, I think. You can eat as much bacon and eggs and steak and cheese as a lumberjack, according to him. But you can't touch any of the interesting foods, like doughnuts or cookies or Coke.

I woke with a wonderful feeling, like I was on top of a mountain, and down below, the whole world was mine. Even though my eyes were closed I was smiling, remembering David and the night before, and seeing the day we planned ahead, and beyond that—one whole month more of freedom before school began.

Oh, maybe not complete freedom. I was working twenty hours a week in Westwood, at 31 Flavors. Just enough hours so the days weren't boring.

It was Wednesday, my day off. David and I were going to the beach together. We'd arranged it on the way home, after the movie last night. But there was still plenty of time before I had to get up. David wouldn't be meeting me until after noon. He worked mornings, and again in the late afternoons till dark, when ladies were home. David's a Fuller Brush man. The hours are good, and his time's his own. He's only eighteen, but I can't *believe* how much money he's put away for college.

I heard my door open. It was Jeffrey, about to

wake me with his Chinese torture tricks. This time, I decided, I wouldn't flinch. No matter how much he tickled, I would bear it like a Spartan.

"Hey, Andrea? You awake?" he whispered from the foot of my bed. "Come on. Get up! It's nearly nine thirty!"

I didn't answer.

"Hey . . . you know what . . . I counted them again. There are thirty-seven. That's two more than last month!"

He was talking about his warts. He worries about them a lot. Both hands are covered with them. My mother says they'll go away, that she had some when she was young, too, but that you outgrow them. Instead of answering him, I let out a soft, sighing sound, like you do when you're fast asleep, and turned over so he couldn't see my face.

Jeff's nearly ten and a pretty neat kid, considering everything. On a skateboard he's as graceful as a champion surfer. The way he talks about me to his friends, it's like I was Miss Teenage America. It's positively embarrassing.

"Andrea! Come on! Mom wants you to help me weed, and it's getting hot already." He tugged lightly at the sheet blanket, but I had it tucked firmly under my legs.

"Okay! You asked for it!" He laughed his villain's laugh and, with one hard yank, uncovered my feet so he could begin the torture.

There's a secret to withstanding the Chinese tickle torture. I learned it through trial and error.

When I used to laugh and cry and beg for mercy, the torturer (usually my sister, Sue), would keep it up longer. But as soon as I learned to block it out, to set my mind to thinking about something else, I took the fun out of it for her. And pretty soon, she'd give up and let me sleep some more.

In about a minute, Jeff got tired of tickling and came to the side of my bed to see if I was really asleep.

That's when I jumped up and pulled him down on the bed to give him a taste of his own medicine.

We were laughing and screaming and making so much noise that pretty soon Mom came in. "Okay! Andrea . . . Jeff! That's enough! You can hear the two of you all over the neighborhood!" She pulled us apart. "Get up, Andrea, and come in for breakfast. And Jeff. You get outside and start that weeding."

Mother was kneading dough for whole wheat bread when I came into the kitchen. She says there are all kinds of preservatives in store-bought breads, so she bakes her own, putting in wheat germ and honey and all kinds of stuff that's supposed to be good for you. Actually, it's kind of fun making bread, punching the dough down and turning it and pushing it with the heel of your hand. Gets rid of your aggressions, Dad says. And there's nothing better than the smell of bread baking.

I got out the pitcher of orange juice and poured what was left—about an ounce—into the glass. My mother must have eyes in back of her head, because she couldn't even see what I was doing, but she said, "Make yourself some more."

"Must we have Michael Jackson on *all* the time?" I complained. I took a can of orange juice from the freezer and peeled off the cap.

Mother reached a floured hand to the volume-knob and turned the radio down. Then she leaned into the dough and went on kneading. "What time'd you get home last night?" she asked.

I carefully measured three cans of water into the pitcher and started breaking up the frozen lump. "About midnight." The inquisition was beginning. Every time I went out with David lately, I had to account for every minute.

"More like one o'clock," Mom said, giving me a quick look on her way to the bread pans.

If she knew what time I got home, why did she ask? But it was too nice a day to let her get to me, so I didn't answer back. I was nearly sixteen and figured it was about time she trusted me. If fifteen years of training hadn't sunk in yet, it sure wouldn't now. "He picked me up after work and we decided to catch the ten o'clock show at the Bruin, and then we came *straight* home." I emphasized the *straight*, so she'd get the idea. "I didn't even ask him in for a Coke."

"You know I told you I don't want you home after midnight during the week," my mother said. "And I don't think you should be seeing so much of David either. Every night like that."

"Like what?" I asked. "And why not?" I knew full well why she thought not. She'd told me often enough before. I poured myself a full glass of juice, refrigerated the rest and went into the family room. Her hassling was not going to ruin my day. I started hunting for the View section of the *Times.* Breakfast always tasted better if I had Doonesbury, Mary Worth, and Dear Abby to look forward to.

My mother sighed and opened the oven to put the bread in to rise. A minute later she came into the family room with a cup of coffee, sat down at the table, and peered over the cup at me. "You *know* perfectly well why not, Andrea," she said. "I don't agree with these mothers who give their daughters the Pill when they're still wet behind the ears. I don't think it's good for a young girl to be intimate so early with any young man who looks at her twice."

"Oh, Mom!" I groaned. I could feel my face grow hot. "I'm not on the Pill, and I'm not planning to sleep around . . . and besides, David and I are not . . ." I stopped. I caught a flash of red T-shirt passing by. Jeff was eavesdropping again.

My mother saw him, too. "Why aren't you out weeding?" she asked irritably. "Now go on, Jeff. I want all that crabgrass out of the dichondra today!"

"I just came in for a . . . peach. . . ." Jeff said. It was obvious he had only thought of the peach at the last minute. He was stalling, hoping to hear some more.

So my mother switched the conversation. "What

āre your plans for today?" She watched Jeff so that he'd leave faster.

"The beach. I'm meeting David around twelve thirty, and we're going to Santa Monica." On the spur of the moment I added, "And maybe to UCLA afterwards. There's a special art show he wants to see." David had mentioned the exhibit, but he hadn't said anything about seeing it today. I don't know why I added that, maybe to show Mom that we didn't spend all our time just "mooning at each other" (her words).

"I thought his mother needed the car in the afternoon. . . ."

"She does." I had found Dear Abby and wās trying to concentrate, but it's not easy when your mother is asking you questions at the same time.

"Then how are you getting there and back?" she wanted to know. "Not hitchhiking, I hope!"

I looked up, annoyed now. I can't think how many times I'd heard her lecture on *that* subject. And it was so ridiculous. All the kids I knew hitched. Whenever I'd tell my mother that, she'd just say, "I don't care what *all* the kids do. I only care what *you* do, and I don't want *you* hitching. No matter what!"

"How are you getting to the beach, then?" my mother asked. That's another thing about my mother. Once she gets an idea in her head, she's like a dog with a bone. Doesn't let go till the bone's stark clean.

"Bus . . ." I said with a deep, annoyed sigh. All

this hassle over a little trip to the beach. I wondered what she'd do if I really were a rebel. I poured some oat flakes into a bowl, added milk, then tried to get back to Dear Abby.

"Good," Mother said. "And watch yourself on the bus, too. Just the other day I read about . . ." She saw I wasn't really listening, so she just added, "You just can't be careful enough these days."

She got up to take her cup to the sink. I watched her retreating back and shook my head. Mothers! You'd think the whole world was a snake pit, the way mine talked. "Be sure to lock the door when you go out. Don't talk to strange men. Be home by dark. Be careful of this. Don't do that." I couldn't understand why she worried so. Nothing had ever happened in our neighborhood.

Well, maybe that's what happens to people when they get older. They get more cautious. I wasn't scared of anything, and I wasn't going to be. As far as I was concerned, the world was out there waiting—like a big, red, juicy apple. And I could hardly wait to taste every bit of it.

2

Mom had said I should help Jeff. So for the next hour and a half I was out there with him, weeding and sweating. After that I showered and washed my hair before getting into my swimsuit. Then I stood in front of the mirror and looked myself over, trying to see what other people saw when they looked at me, how David saw me.

On the minus side, The Bod. Ukk. I turned this way and that, noting the faults. Legs a little too long. Hips a bit too much. Waist the same. Bosom, B minus. In short, I looked something like a stick. Mom says she didn't fill out till she was nearly seventeen. Do *I* have to wait so long?

On the plus side, nice hair. Thick, long, and honey-blonde. Skin—not bad. A zit now and then, especially early in the summer when I snacked on the job (Oh, Mocha Almond Fudge!). But today, my skin was clear and a nice rosy color.

Eyes—brown with thick, long lashes (inherited

from Dad)—no better, no worse than anyone else's, though David seems to think otherwise. Once, he held my face in his hands and looked at me with this serious look of his and said, "Those eyes . . . they don't hide anything!"

"*Anything?*" I asked, feeling my face flush and hearing my voice crack. "God, I hope not!"

I grinned, remembering, and decided to borrow Sue's new bikini. Maybe it would make what was small look a little bigger, and what was big, a little smaller. It was chartreuse, with little pink-and-white flowers. My own suit was two years old and I didn't want to buy another until the late summer sales.

"No you don't," my mother said when I came into the kitchen to find some colored yarn to tie back my hair. "You just go right back and take that off. Susan paid hard-earned money for that suit, and she has the right to be the first to wear it."

So I went back and changed to my old blue-and-white, then put on jeans and a pink cotton blouse. One more look in the mirror. If David's going to love me, I decided, it would have to be for my mind, not my bod.

I saw David before he saw me. He was leaning against the bus-stop bench, head bent over a paperback. God, he's skinny, I thought, wanting to hug that tall, narrow body. When you run ten miles a day for your high school track team, I guess you can't help being thin. I ran the last few steps and put a hand on his arm.

David looked up from his book and grinned. I thought for the dozenth time since the night before how much I loved him.

Last night. It had been like magic, like maybe it can only be in California. Cool, with an orange-blossom fragrance. The smog had moved out with the heat about five o'clock, and the sky sparkled with a trillion stars. I guess the word for it is balmy, like the night was a pillow to snuggle into.

When we got home from the movie in Westwood, David parked. "It's late. I better go in," I whispered. It seemed wrong to speak in normal tones, somehow.

David took my hand and walked me to the door. My father had left the hall light on, and through the glass next to the door, there was enough light for me to see David. His face had this real soft look when he bent to kiss me. With that look, and the magic of the night, a warm, happy sweetness oozed through me.

I don't know how long we stood there kissing, because after a while I wasn't aware of anything except how good I felt, and how I never wanted to stop. But suddenly it was like a bell going off in my head, shocking me away from that delicious place I'd been. "No, David," I whispered, pulling away and taking his hand from under my shirt. "Don't."

For a while he just held me and I could feel his heart hammering against my chest. He didn't speak for a long time. Then, when he did, his voice was very low. "I love you, Andrea. It can't be wrong." He traced his finger over my cheek and I melted, I was afraid my legs would give way.

Mother thinks I don't listen to her, but she's wrong. Her words were a brick wall between David and me. He stood on one side, and I on the other. No matter what he might say, or how I might feel, I had to wait, keep that barrier between us until I was older, maybe much older. I swallowed and looked down at the button on his shirt because it was so hard talking of this without feeling embarrassed.

"I'd better go in," I said softly. I turned and unlocked the door.

"Tomorrow?" he asked, as if he thought what he'd done might make a difference, might have angered me so I'd not want to see him again. "The beach? Bus stop around noon?"

"Oh, yes," I said, reaching up and kissing him on the cheek. "Oh, yes. Tomorrow."

The bus to the beach was hot and crowded, and the beach was hot and crowded, with heat waves shimmering in the distance. We took off our shoes and ran. The sand was burning and we stopped at little oases of shade, under someone's umbrella or near a wastebasket.

Finally we settled on a square of sand just above the wet shore. We dropped our things and peeled off our clothes almost in the same instant, we were so eager to get into the ocean and cool our scorched feet.

Undressed, with only my bikini, I felt suddenly

naked and crossed my arms over my B-minus chest, remembering what David had tried to do the night before. But he didn't seem to notice. Stripped to his trunks, he took off at a run toward the water. "Last one in's a two-toed sloth!" he called as he went plowing into the icy surf.

Then we ran down the beach. I tried to keep up with David, who would run ahead, then come back and almost run in place while he chided me on being so slow. Afterward, we lay on our towel. Panting from the run, but bubblingly happy, I was ready to spend the next hour baking to that golden brown every southern California kid aims for before school starts.

"People are mean," David said, rolling over onto his stomach and leaning his head on one hand so he could see me.

I opened my eyes a slit, then closed them. Without sunglasses, the glare was ferocious. "They are not . . ." I said. "They're wonderful. The whole world is wonderful."

He dropped warm sand on my stomach and I opened my eyes only long enough to give him a warning look.

"Okay, they're kind. They're sweet," David agreed. "Like the sweet, kind people I met today."

"Tell me." I rolled over on my stomach the better to toast my back and turned my face to him.

"I rang the bell to this house, okay? The lady comes to the door and I say, 'Fuller Brush man,' and she opens the door a crack. 'Which of these free samples would you like,' I ask, holding out my precious samples, which, by the way, I have to pay dearly for. She grabs two brushes and is about to slam the door when I hear her husband in the background. He yells, 'Go git 'im, Blackie! Go on— *kill!*' I hear this horse galloping toward the door and pretty soon there he is, fangs bared, a gigantic German shepherd snarling at me like he hasn't eaten in a week!"

"Oh, wow!" I said. He often told me horror stories like this, and I really thought he was pretty brave, sticking it out.

David went on. "The lady says, 'I don't buy no door-to-door stuff.' And then she shuts the door on me."

"Poor baby," I sympathized, teasing. "Maybe you'd be better off scooping ice cream at two-sixty an hour, huh?" I dripped a fistful of sand on his neck.

He grabbed my hand and growled like a mad dog and suddenly we were laughing and tussling like puppies. To escape him I ran for the water, but he followed and splashed me. Pretty soon we were both in the wet sand, laughing so hard we were crying. "Say it! Say it!" I commanded, holding a fist of wet sand over his head. "People are wonderful! Say it!"

"You're right! You're right! People are great! The whole world's wonderful! Only don't drop that!"

I laughed and dropped it anyway, then scrambled out of his way, racing for the beach towel. From there, giggling with excitement and fear of retaliation, I watched while he started to come after me. But he didn't. Instead, he dove into the first wave and weaved in and out of the water like a porpoise, surfacing far out and swimming with strong, clean strokes. "He's so beautiful," I thought, and watched with a bursting sense of joy.

I suppose, looking back, if I hadn't dropped the sand into David's hair so that he had to take extra time to swim it out, we wouldn't have missed the bus. And having missed the bus, we wouldn't have taken the extra forty minutes at McDonald's, stuffing ourselves with two Big Macs each. Which put us at the bus stop just as the next bus, three minutes early, disappeared around the corner.

We stood there looking at each other, annoyed at the rapid transit and ourselves for not having hurried out of McDonald's, and then I said, "Let's hitch."

"You said your mother doesn't want you to," David said.

"I know. But you're with me. And the next bus doesn't come for another half hour. Even then, we still have to change in Westwood. Besides, you have to work later."

"I would like to get in a few hours tonight," David said, looking at his watch.

"Anyway," I said, completing my argument, "if we get a quick ride, I won't even have to phone about being late."

David looked doubtful.

"Listen, Dave. If we have to wait for buses, it'll

be two hours before we get back. My mother will think we've been . . . you know what." My eyes fluttered suggestively.

"Oh, you . . ." David said laughing. He took my arm. "Okay . . . we'll hitch."

3

So, there we were, David and I, on the corner of Wilshire Boulevard and Third Street with our thumbs out. It was nearly six when the first car stopped. It was an old Chevy, and the driver was black. David leaned in through the open front window and asked, "Going to the Valley? We're trying to get to Encino."

"Sorry, man," the guy said. "I'm headed downtown."

The next car that stopped was a green Dodge. Looking back, I'd put it in the conservative category—safe. When David asked the driver if he was going toward Encino, the guy said, "Sure. Hop in. I'm going right by."

David opened the door and let me go first, putting me right next to the driver. I looked at him and he seemed a nice enough guy. Blue sport shirt. Haircut like they wore in World War II movies, like a brush with half-inch bristles. He smiled in my direction, then looked away.

"Say, thanks a lot," David said, getting in and slamming the door. "If we hadn't lucked into you, we might have had to wait for the bus and we'd be late getting home."

"You kids been to the beach?" the man asked, checking his rearview mirror and then pulling out into traffic.

"How'd you guess?" I asked, laughing.

David's legs were a pink-purple. He said, "Boy, Andrea. Are you going to hurt tonight!"

For a few miles, we drove in silence. I started to think of my mother's warnings, and then thought how silly she was. We were getting home so quickly this way. The man had turned onto the Santa Monica Freeway and soon we'd be on the San Diego, and then the Ventura, and then voilà . . .! I began to relax and think of the riddles we'd been making up in McDonald's.

I nudged David. "Hey, let me see that sheet." I was referring to a list we'd made of words like monster, witch, King Kong, and so on. Dave pulled it from his wallet and we leaned together studying it.

"I've got one!" I cried. "What kind of gorilla lives in China?"

David thought awhile then asked, "What?"

"*Hong* Kong!"

David laughed and the driver kind of snorted. Then David said, "What do you call the parents of ghosts and goblins?"

"I give up," I said.

David looked like he was bursting. "Dead . . . and Mummy . . ."

"Oh, *David!*" I exploded.

It was like that all the way to Encino. We were completely wrapped up in our own games, finding it such fun that the miles just flew by and we hardly noticed the driver, or even realized that he wasn't laughing. When we got off the freeway at Hayvenhurst, I realized where we were. "Wait! Stop!" I cried. "David lives on the next block. We can get off here."

The man pulled over, just as I asked. "Thanks," I said. I slipped over in the seat to get out. "I only live about a mile from here. You can go right back on the freeway if you turn around here."

"Well, if it's only a mile, I'll be glad to take you the rest of the way," he said. "I don't mind."

"Gee, would you?" I slipped back into the car. "That would be great! I'm already later than I said I'd be. My mother is a king-size worrier."

"No problem. It's only a couple of blocks, hardly out of my way at all."

"Maybe I'd better go along," David spoke softly, so only I'd hear. "To see you home."

I glanced at the driver. He was looking straight ahead. He seemed so normal, so okay. "Don't be silly," I told David. "You've got to go to work, anyway. I'll be okay."

"Sure?" David sounded doubtful.

"Come on, now," I chided. "You sound like my mother!"

That convinced him. He thanked the man, patted my sunburned arm so that I flinched, and said he'd call me. I remember looking back and seeing him blow me a kiss.

"I live just across Ventura," I said, settling into the seat David had vacated. "Just keep going down Hayvenhurst. I'll tell you where to turn."

"Right." The driver held the wheel with two hands, not looking my way at all.

He was driving a little faster than he should have, considering Hayvenhurst isn't all that wide and he didn't know where I lived. But I didn't think much of it. I figured he was in a hurry to get home. "You turn right at Adlon," I said, about a block before the turn. "That's the next right."

But instead of slowing down, he picked up speed and turned on the radio. Suddenly we were passing Adlon.

"Hey, wait a minute!" I said, feeling the first quiver of fear. "You passed my street!"

"Oh, sorry. Guess I was going too fast. I'll turn at the next street."

But he didn't. I watched the houses fly by and began to worry. If he didn't slow down soon, we'd be headed for the hills. A lump formed in my throat. What's going on? I thought. Why's he doing this? Was he crazy? Didn't he know he was scaring me?

A few blocks further he took a left and, instead of turning, accelerated up the hill.

"Hey, wait a minute . . ." I could hardly get the words out. "Where are we going? Please, mister . . . just turn around in that driveway! I have to get home!" My hands got cold and wet. It was hard keeping my voice from sounding hysterical.

He didn't answer. He glanced my way once, pale eyes kind of glazed, focused somewhere around my middle. Oh God, I thought! It's not a mistake. He *is* crazy. It's the Hillside Strangler; the papers were filled with stories about some man who had killed eight girls. Was I going to be the ninth? Was he going to drive me up into the hills and kill me? I pressed my body hard against the door and grabbed the handle. Sounds started coming from my throat, like I was strangling. In a minute I'd be sobbing.

Stop it, I told myself. Get hold of yourself. Think! Maybe he wants money. Keep calm! I cleared my throat a couple of times, but it didn't help much. "My parents would pay you . . . if that's what you want. . . ." Again he ignored me. All he did was drive, eyes forward, hands gripping the steering wheel so the knuckles were white, like he was in a world all his own.

"Mister, please!" I cried. "You better get me home now. This isn't one bit funny! My boyfriend said he'd call home to see if I arrived okay!" The words were so brave, so threatening, and they sounded so false even to my ears.

"Shut up! Just do as I say and you'll get home!" he snapped.

Do as he says. What did he mean? What did he expect *me* to do? I began to look for a way to escape. If I opened the car door, I could jump out. But the car was going so fast! I was afraid! Oh, God, I thought . . . someone help me!

I saw a kid my brother's age come skateboarding down the winding road. I started to open the window to scream out to him, but I couldn't get it down fast enough, and the wind must have carried my scream away because as the boy passed, he waved at me and grinned.

The driver turned an ugly face to me. He swatted me hard across the mouth with the back of his hand. I started to cry, scrunching myself into the door away from him, trying to make myself as small a target as possible. "Do that again," he warned, showing me a gun I hadn't seen before, "and you'll never get home."

"Please, please," I begged, between sobs. "I promise I won't tell. Just take me home. Please!"

He didn't answer.

"Oh, mister. Don't *do* this. I never hurt anyone. *Please*, take me home!"

"Shut up!" he said.

My teeth began chattering. I was so sick with fear, so cold, that I could hardly think. It didn't seem possible this could be happening to me. It had to be a nightmare. Any minute now I'd wake up. Any minute he'd change his mind and turn back. What was I going to do?

Meanwhile we were passing all these nice suburban homes. Husbands were coming home from work, pulling into driveways. Gardeners were busy clipping hedges and mowing lawns. All this life was going on, and we were going by, and no one saw. No one knew what was happening to me!

It must have been a half hour that we drove around in the hills, careening around corners too fast for me to escape, and driving always into less and less populated streets. Finally, he pulled off onto a dirt road, drove a ways, then cut the motor.

My hand was on the door handle even before the car pulled to a stop, but he had anticipated it. He grabbed my arm and yanked me next to him. I tried to push away, but as soon as he cut the motor, he had both hands free. He smacked me again and then pointed the gun.

"Out!"

"Please, oh please don't kill me! Please let me go!" I begged.

"Out!" He grabbed my hair and forced my head back. "Do as I say, and you won't get hurt." He led me, dragged me, really, out of the car.

There was no time to think. Yet I remember looking frantically for signs of people, cars, a house nearby. But there was nothing. Just a lot of rocks and weeds, a thicket of bushes, and some trees.

He pulled me along, yanking me through prickly bushes. The dry branches caught on my shirt and tore it. I was sobbing, begging him to let me go. Not once did he answer. Not once did he look me in the eye.

When we got to a clearing, hidden from the road by bushes, he waved the gun at me. Oh, God,

I thought. Now. He's going to kill me. I don't want to die!

I stared at the barrel and started to shiver. My head tumbled with crazy thoughts. Run. Fight. Scream. Beg. Anything to keep alive another few moments.

"Undress!" he ordered suddenly.

My eyes flew from the gun to his face. It was pale, like someone who never went outdoors, with two bright spots of red on the cheeks. His thin, wet lips were fixed in a small smile. Oh, God, I thought . . . *that*? I backed away, but he grabbed my arm and yanked at my blouse. "You heard me! Hurry up!" He put the gun on a rock out of reach and began to take off his pants.

Like a robot, like someone in a dream, I did as he said. But I was trembling so that my fingers wouldn't undo the button on my jeans. "Don't do this to me . . . I've never . . . Please . . . Don't! Not that!" I begged.

He whopped me again on the side of the head and shoved me to the ground. I cried out as a sharp rock cut into my hip. And then, he came down on top of me.

It was so awful, so hurtful. Inside I was scream-ing, *Daddy, save me. Mommy . . . I'll never dis-obey you again. God, please. I'll never doubt You again. I'll be the best person in the world, if You'll only make this stop. Please, someone! Help me!*

But nobody came to help, nobody came to save me. Nobody heard my cries.

Sometime during it all, I lunged for the gun.

But he got to it first. Then he held it to my head and asked, "Are you worth a five-cent bullet? Are you, you cheap, rotten bitch?"

Staring up into his flushed, mad face, I didn't know what to say. What would be the right answer? For the first time since it had all begun, I felt calm though. *The Chinese tickle torture.* That would be the only way to survive this. Tune out the hurt, keep my wits about me. Memorize everything about that face so it would be branded in my head for eternity. I started to study him, the way his eyes were set, the mole near the ear, the teeth. Under the crew cut, an inch-long scar. Keep your mind on things like that, I thought.

"Answer me!" he shouted, clicking the safety off the gun. "Are you worth a five-cent bullet?"

"No. No," I whispered, hoping it was the right answer.

Later I remembered seeing a lizard skitter away into a bush, and it was like seeing through a dark glass. It wasn't me seeing it; it was someone else, and I was dreaming it. I didn't feel anything then, only a big emptiness inside, like I'd never feel anything again—pain, joy, sorrow—anything.

"Get up!" he ordered at last. "Get dressed!" I turned toward him and couldn't quite focus on his face. But I did what he said. Part of me began thinking, he'll kill me now. I'll never see my family again. That's it. He's done with me, and I can identify him. But it didn't matter. I didn't much care. Maybe it would end the nightmare.

"In the car! Come on, move!"

I stumbled over the brush, half dragged, half pushed, and was almost thrown into the car. Then, while I sat stunned, empty, seeing nothing, recording nothing, he drove off. Along the way he began talking. "I'm sorry. I don't know why I do it. I've got a wife, two kids. I'm sorry, really. I'm sorry. . . ."

Much good that does, I thought numbly. I couldn't bear to even look his way. Much good that does.

Somewhere along Hayvenhurst he slowed. As he pulled off the road, he gave me instructions. The voice was cold again, threatening. "You keep this to yourself, understand? You tell the police or anyone, and I'll be back. I know where you live!" Then, while the car was still in motion, he said, "Out! And don't forget what I said!"

I didn't need to be told twice. Dust and gravel sprayed over me as I hit the ground. The car spun off the gravel, picked up speed, and in seconds disappeared around a bend.

I don't know how long I sat there, scratched, hurting, numb, but finally I got up and, like someone in a trance, began walking.

4

I guess I must have looked a sight, trudging along that shoulder of the road. If people in cars saw me, I wasn't aware. It wasn't until much later that I got a good look at myself and saw what they would have seen. My face was scratched and marked with dried-up, tear-stained dirt tracks. My hair was full of leaves and twigs and fell wildly over my eyes, even into my mouth. My blouse was ripped, and my jeans were muddy. My whole being seemed to be concentrated around the searing pain between my legs. I wanted to get home, get into my room, wash myself, then lock myself away from the whole world.

Later I would kick myself for not having the sense to look back when he took off. Why did I care about his threats? What worse thing could he have done to me, after all? But I didn't look back, didn't get his license number. I was too stunned.

I don't know how long I'd been walking when the crunch of tires on gravel startled me back to reality. *It's him,* I thought. Oh God! He's back! My heart lurched, and my mind switched on like a room suddenly flooded with light: Run! Get away! *Scream!*

"Andrea! *Andrea!*" An arm grabbed me from behind and swung me around. "Andrea? What's wrong?"

I struck at the body, hitting blindly, screaming all the time until I realized it was Kim. And then I clutched at her, digging my fingers into her arm, and began to tremble. It was as if I had been plunged into a lake of ice water and was standing nude in below-zero winds.

"Andrea, what happened?" Kim repeated. Shivering, teeth chattering, I could only shake my head as she led me to the car.

The girls inside were from my school. They had seen me as they passed, turned around, and come up behind. Kim was a friend, the daughter of my high school swim coach. Karen was on the tennis team with me. I didn't know the third girl. They sat there in the car, watching me, wanting to know.

"Please, take me home," I whispered. "I just want to go home." It seemed like the smell of him was all over me. Surely the girls had to notice it. I couldn't look at them.

"But what happened? You look awful! Who hurt you?" Kim asked. She smoothed back my hair.

"I was . . ." I couldn't bring myself to say the

shameful thing. I stared down at my hands. "I was . . . I was . . ." I started to cry. They let me cry and just sat there, not starting the car, just sitting there and watching me. I think they all knew, that it was no surprise, really, when I brought myself finally to say those awful words. . . . "*I was raped!*"

"Oh, Andrea!" they said in unison. "How awful!" Kim sounded appalled. "You poor kid! How?"

I told them as little as possible. Huddled within myself with my legs drawn up tightly, I became terribly aware of the warm wetness and the cutting pain between them.

The girl in the driver's seat started the car. "We'll take you to the police. They'll know what to do."

"No! He *warned* me!" I grabbed for the door handle. "Let me out! Please, I don't want anybody to know!" Then, I began to realize how much *they* already knew. "Promise! Promise!" I screamed. "Don't tell anyone!"

Kim put a hand on my arm, but I shook it away. All I could think was that I'd already told someone, that if it went further, he'd know. He'd kill me.

"We won't tell, Andrea. Calm down. Don't worry. But listen, Cindy's right. We should go to the police. If you wait much longer, he'll get away. If you can give them a description of his car and all, maybe they can still pick him up, before he's out of Encino."

Oh, how I wanted to go home, to get into a bath

and soak off all the filth. To get into my bed and bury my head under the blankets and sleep for the rest of eternity. How could I face police now, men police, while I was hurting like this, unwashed, so ashamed. How could I talk to anyone about it, for surely, going to the police meant having to tell everything.

"No, no, please . . . just take me home," I sobbed. But the girls wouldn't hear of it. There was no doubt at all, they said, that the best thing to do, the only logical thing, was to go straight to the police. From there, of course, I could phone home.

In the end, they got their way. For who was I at that time to buck such logic? Kim, arm around my shoulder, spoke soothing words. In the front seat the other two girls whispered together, glancing at me from time to time with worried faces. And all the while the car moved forward, against my wishes, toward the police station.

In the station, Kim and the girls led me like a lost child, first to Information, where an officer told them what to do, then down a hall to an elevator, and finally, to the proper room. Around me there were voices, people going by, looking at me. I wished a hole would open up and swallow me.

A policewoman took the first report. She was trim and pretty, in her thirties, and I couldn't quite look her in the eye. She told the girls to wait in the hall and took me to a chair opposite a desk. "Sit down. There are some questions I have to ask.

I know you'd rather not answer questions now, but it's important, while the details are fresh."

"Please, could I go to the bathroom first?" I needed so badly to wash up.

"Not till the doctor sees you, I'm sorry. When there's a rape, you might destroy the evidence."

I was dazed and I didn't know what she meant. My eyes wandered to the water cooler. "Could I have a glass of water then?"

"No, not that either. I'm terribly sorry, but if there's been oral copulation . . . well, the doctor will want to get semen specimens."

Tears slid down my face, and I wiped them away with my fists. Words like *semen* and *oral copulation* were so strange to me. They were secret words, not to be spoken easily, especially in public. And what was this about doctors? Would I be examined? Was someone going to poke around in my private places where I already hurt so much?

Suddenly I just didn't care if they caught him or not. I got up and started to walk away. The officer came after me and put her hand out. "Where are you going?"

"Home."

"You can't do that. Now come on and sit down. I know it's hard. But you had the courage to come in and report this, so let's get some details so we can get this out on the wires." She brought me back to the chair and made me sit down. Then she returned to her seat and leaned across the desk and studied me, measured me, like she was trying to decide what kind of person I was. "If you've really been raped, surely you'll want to give us a description of your attacker and whatever information you can to help us catch him. You do want him apprehended, don't you? Not only to punish him for what he did to you but to prevent him from hurting someone else."

All I heard in that long speech was the word *if.* "What do you mean . . . *if*?" I cried. "For heaven's sake, don't you believe me?"

"Sit down!" the officer repeated. "Now listen to me. I didn't say I don't believe you. But now and then a girl comes in and cries rape when there hasn't been a rape . . . and she seems just as sincere as you. Just last week we had a case like that. A fourteen-year-old girl accused two boys of attacking her. The boys were put in Juvenile Hall. The next day the girl admitted she lied. Do you get the picture?" The policewoman's eyes never left my face. "Sometimes a girl gets mad at her boyfriend and cries rape. You understand? We just have to be sure." Her voice softened. "Andrea. Tell me what happened."

5

Right after the policewoman took the preliminary report, they let me call home. I used a phone at one of the desks, and turned my back on the other people in the room where I dialed. The phone rang twice and then I heard my brother's voice.

"Jeffrey?" I said, hearing my tone a pitch above normal. "Put Mom on."

"Andrea?" Jeff said. "What's the matter. You sound funny. Where are you anyway? It's nearly eight o'clock. You were supposed to be back from the beach by now."

"Just call Mom."

"Mom's not here. She's next door at the Williams's. They have new Irish setter pups. You should see them! They're so little!"

"Jeffrey!" I cut him short. "Get Daddy. Please, please hurry."

"Daddy's gone to the service station. He thinks his fuel pump's conked out or something. He just left. What's the matter?"

I began to have a hysterical feeling now. It must have been an hour, at least, since it happened. I needed so badly to get out of those clothes, to feel the comfort of my mother's arms around me. "Is *Sue* home?" The words hurt my throat.

"Sue's with Mom. Hey, Andrea? What's wrong? You sound funny. Can't you tell me?"

No I couldn't, but I couldn't say that to Jeff. "Jeff, listen. Go get Mom, right now. *Please!*" If he had said one more thing, asked one more question, I would have broken down.

While I waited for my mother to come to the phone, fearful thoughts tortured me. How would she take it? I needed her support so badly, and usually she was such a comfort. When things went wrong at school, just standing close to her often helped. Would she understand, blame me, be angry? Dad. I was still his little girl, his princess, pure and perfect. I *was.* . . .

I wiped my eyes. It hurt so to think of them, I could hardly bear it. Instead, I made myself picture the bright, friendly kitchen at home where the phone was, the white tile counter with the big bowl of summer fruit on the pass-through. There was a cork bulletin board over the phone with notes like: PICK UP T's SHOES; MONTEREY JACK CHEESE, AVOCADOS, YOGURT, MARGARINE, WHEAT

GERM. The kitchen would have a fresh-bread smell, because by now the dough Mom was kneading in the morning would have been baked.

There was some comfort in imagining those things, in holding on to the security blanket of home.

"Hello? Andrea?" my mother finally said. "Is something wrong? Where are you?" There was suspicion in her voice. Intuition . . . as if she'd guessed. A touch of fear.

"Mom!" I cried. I swallowed the enormous lump in my throat. "I'm at the Encino Police Station. I've been . . . hurt. Please, come quickly."

The Vice Officer, Corbett, led me into this small, plain room away from the main desk where I had given the preliminary report.

He tried to put me at ease, rattling on about how he's a chain smoker and he hoped I didn't mind if he smoked. And I let him rattle on while I focused on the bare, green plaster walls, the small, old wood table, and most of all—the closed door.

"If you'd rather I left the door open," Corbett said, noticing, I guess, that my eyes darted from him to the door a lot. "It's just that I thought you might feel more comfortable in privacy."

I shook my head. "No, that's all right." It wasn't, of course, being alone with him, but it was better than having the door open for everyone to hear.

Then he asked me about school, and my family,

and my interests, trying to put me at ease, I guess.
Finally he said, "This won't be easy. I'm going to
have to ask you things I don't like asking. I don't
mean to offend you. Some of the questions may
be very personal. But I have to ask them." He held
out his pack of cigarettes.

"I don't smoke." I gripped the arms of the chair
and watched him closely. He was a round-faced
man in his middle twenties, and he was dressed in
a brown sport jacket and slacks. He had clicked
on a tape recorder. I was very conscious of the
tape going around slowly, taking down anything
I would say.

"Okay, Andrea. Why don't you start at the beginning. Tell me how it happened."

And so I told him, about going to the beach and
missing the bus and getting the hitch and leaving
David behind when we got to Encino because it
was only another mile to my house. Then I
stopped. My throat got all choked up again, and
my heart began to thump so hard it rang in my
ears. Looking away, I said, "And then he took me
up into the hills somewhere. And he—did it. . . ."

" 'Did it.' You mean—raped you?"

I nodded.

"Have you ever had intercourse before?" Corbett asked.

"No."

Corbett was silent a moment. Maybe he didn't
think I knew what sex was, because the next thing
he asked was, "What precisely did he do?"

I felt sick, like I might throw up. "Do I have to say?"

"I'm sorry, Andrea. This is the hardest part. I told you it wouldn't be easy. Use any words you want. If it's easier for you to use terms like you might read in a textbook, go ahead. Or, if you want to use street language, that's okay, too." He flicked an ash off his cigarette. "But I must know precisely everything he did to you. For example was only rape involved or was there sodomy, too? And oral copulation? Do you understand? Do you know what these things are, what they mean?"

No, I didn't. I suppose I'm retarded in some ways, or *was*. When the girls at school were passing around *The Joy of Sex*, giggling over it in study hall, I was usually doing homework, because after school I had tennis or swimming practice and because, to be honest, I wasn't that interested. I saw some of the illustrations once and they were kind of weird.

I grew up fast that day. Officer Corbett explained what all those words meant, and I actually felt sorry for him. *He* seemed embarrassed. And after he'd described what they meant, and I told him—yes—they had happened to me, he seemed more embarrassed. Apologetic. Ashamed, even. Can you imagine *me* feeling sorry for him?

"Can you describe the car, and anything in it? And the man. Did you learn his name? What did he wear? Any distinguishing features? Did he threaten you with a weapon?"

"The car was green," I said. "I think it was a Dodge. I could ask David." I stopped. No, I couldn't. That would mean David would have to know and I didn't want him to. "I don't know what the man's name was. We didn't ask. But, let's see. I remember some magazines on the front seat when I got in. He threw them in the back."

"What kind of magazines?"

"*Playboy*, I think. Yes. The top one had a picture of a nude woman."

"Anything else?"

"On the way back he kept apologizing. Said he didn't know why he did things like that. He was married, had two kids. . . ."

Corbett nodded. "That's the strange thing about rapists. I've talked with officers who work with them in prison. They say the men are the most normal prisoners there. Often they're married, living normal sex lives at home. In one study I read, *all* the rapists interviewed had available sexual relationships. Furthermore, most rapes are planned in advance. The victim is often staked out, carefully chosen."

"You mean he chose me? Picked me? But why?" I cried. "Maybe I did something to encourage him! Oh, why didn't he go to his wife! Why didn't I listen to my mother! Why didn't I listen to David! He didn't want me to go on alone!"

A man opened the door and looked in. "Mr. and Mrs. Cranston are here," he said. My parents! A cramp of fear rushed through me. "Thanks, Bill. Say, would you bring us some Cokes?" Corbett dug into his pants and flipped the man two quarters. Then the door closed, and he turned back to me.

"Don't start laying on the guilt, Andrea. What happened to you could happen to anyone. I've known of eighty-year-old ladies who have been attacked. Last month we had a case of a girl about your age. She was just walking down the street in broad daylight, and this guy comes up behind and puts his arm around her neck and pulls her into his van." Corbett took a deep drag on his cigarette. "I know another case. This gal pulls into a supermarket parking lot just after it closed. A guy comes over to her and says his car's disabled at the other end of the lot, did she have a jumper cable? She's a trusting kid. Never thought not to help someone in trouble. So she follows the guy to where she expects his car to be and, next thing you know, he sticks a knife to her throat and gets into her car and there you have it." Corbett handed me the Coke the officer brought in. "So don't blame yourself. It wasn't your fault. You didn't ask for it."

I started to shiver. Suddenly it seemed as if there was no place that would be safe anymore. How blind, how naive I'd been, going about the world as if it was my own private playground. It wasn't. David had been right after all, about people. People *were* mean. It was ugly out there, dangerous, with predatory animals roaming the streets, even in daylight.

Corbett removed his jacket and put it around

my shoulders, but I couldn't stop shaking. "Come on, Andrea," he said kindly. "I know it's rough, but we only need a little more, then you can see your parents and go home."

How much more? I wanted to ask. Corbett seemed to read my mind, because he said, "The doctor's next. Then I'd like you to look at some pictures, while it's all fresh in your mind. Hold on, kid. Just a little longer."

A little longer. People always use words like that to string you along beyond what you think you can bear. David says his track coach talks like that. "Okay, you guys. Just once more around. . . ." And then when you've given all you've got left, the coach says, "You deadbeats! Take that lap again!"

That's how it was for me. It was almost 10 P.M. already, and I kept yawning big, deep, sob-filled gulps of air. I wanted to scream, "Enough! No more!" But it wasn't up to me. I was on a roller coaster, and not able to get off, no matter how dizzy I felt, not until the someone in control decided it was time.

6

Whispering. Outside my bedroom door.

Mother: "You're not to disturb her, hear?"

Jeffrey (louder): "But why? She's always up by now!"

Mother: "Sssh!"

Jeffrey (softer): "What happened to Andrea, Mom? Is she okay?"

"Just don't ask questions, Jeffrey. Now do as you're told. And while you're at it, see if you can get those noisy skateboard friends of yours to go ride somewhere else!"

The words fade, moving toward the kitchen. The front door closes. Jeffrey, leaving. Then silence. Not even the comforting, British voice of Michael Jackson through the walls.

I lie in bed, just being. Outside my window, the leaves of the elm tree are motionless in the hot, breathless morning. The doves of yesterday repeat their calls, sad, mournful cries. Down the block the buzz-saw hum of a power mower. Concentrate on that. Don't think.

Loud rock music blasts suddenly, then is turned lower. "For Christ's sake, Sue! Turn that down!" My father's voice. So he's home. And Sue. I close my eyes.

A wave of dizziness washes over me. I pull my knees up close to my chest, cross my arms and turn to my side. Concentrate on something fixed: the Janis Joplin poster on the wall. The white ruffled eyelit canopy over my bed. The Escher calendar. No, not that. Its strange stairways that go up, but seem to go down only make me more sick. *Could I be pregnant?* God, please—no! You don't get morning sickness this soon after, do you?

The doctor's words came back to me from last night, helping cool the fear. "The morning-after pill . . . may have side effects . . . nausea . . . vomiting . . . a few days. . ."

The doctor. A flash of heat rushes over me, leaving me wet with sweat. Me, who hadn't undressed for a doctor since I was ten. Me, who got red all the way down to my toes at the thought, who kept healthy out of fear of the revolting alternative. Suddenly to have all that tender modesty yanked away a second time in one day. There I was on an examining table under bright lights, with only a sheet to cover my nakedness. My legs were spread, and my heels were in stirrups. And this strange man doctor was touching and prying and pushing cold metal objects into me, saying, "Relax . . . relax . . . I don't want to hurt you."

Relax. My hands were icy and wet. My heart was pounding and my throat hurt with the effort of not crying. It was one last, unbearable indignity. And words flowed over and around me, words about the possibility of V.D., pregnancy, abortions, and of other infection.

Stop it! Block it out! Get up, have your breakfast, and don't talk about it or think about it. Do something, anything, that will keep your head too busy to think.

The head is free when you're washing your face or brushing your hair. Usually, I do those things so automatically that ten minutes later it's hard to remember if I've done them. Not today. Today I deliberately put all my attention into spreading the half inch of Pepsodent on the toothbrush. Then I look in the mirror and move the brush up and down like the dentist says you should. For a second my eyes look back, then quickly dart away. There's a look in them I don't want to examine. As long as I can put great attention into these routine things, the mind will be too busy to think.

But the ruse doesn't work so well. There comes a moment when the face in the mirror does look back. My hand stops brushing my hair and the face blends into his and then into last night at the police station.

"First," Corbett said, "I'll give you this book of facial shapes. See if you can come up with one shape that seems closest to his."

There must have been a thousand pictures, of noses and eyes and ears and lips. Of cheekbones, high and low. And then I had to decide just where, on what shaped face, each thing went. You'd be surprised how much difference a quarter inch makes in terms of how far apart eyes are, or how much of an angle or slant, or where they are in relation to the nose or mouth.

It was hard, keeping what he looked like clear in my head when there were so many pictures bombarding me with other alternatives. I almost began to doubt the face I thought I'd branded on my memory.

"Andrea . . . dear." It was my mother, framed in the bathroom door, her face in the mirror, beside mine. Our eyes caught and held. I think she must have been watching me for some time before I saw her.

I put the hairbrush down and walked into her arms. We just stood there, my head on her shoulder and she rocked me, as if I were a baby. Then, without a word, she drew me with her into the kitchen.

The night before they hadn't pressed me. I suppose the police filled them in, or else the girls, but anyway, I was in no shape then to talk. Yet as cried-out and exhausted as I was, my fine-tuned antennae were already up, checking. On the drive home they didn't miss Mom's tight-lipped, barely controlled look, or Daddy's red-eyed hurt. I wanted so badly to hear in their voices, see in their faces, that I hadn't changed to them. But when we got home, Mom just said, "We'll talk in the morning." With a hand on my back, she directed me to my room. There was in her manner something I couldn't define and I was too wasted, too out-of-it, to try.

When I entered the kitchen, Dad pulled out a chair as if I were a guest and asked what cereal I wanted.

"None, Dad. Thanks. Just coffee."

"How about an egg then, honey?" Mom asked.

"No. I really don't want anything. Just coffee. Black. I feel a bit queasy."

Mom and Dad exchanged looks and then Mom went for a cup, and Daddy for the coffee. They were practically falling all over each other, they were so eager to do something for me.

Sue came in, looked the scene over, made a disgusted face, and sat down. My sister and I don't always get along. Maybe because we're opposites. Or maybe because she's older by two years and has no patience for disorder or inefficiency, or weakness, things I excel at. I guess she's a perfectionist, while I'm something of a slob. All I have to do is open her closet and breathe, and she can tell I've been there.

"Sleep well?" Sue asked. It looked like *she* hadn't slept very well. Without asking, she got two bowls from the cabinet and put one in front of me. Without asking or looking at me, she dumped some Cheerios into mine before filling hers.

"Not very," I said. I'd slept heavily at first, then

awakened to think *he* was in the room. I locked the windows and pulled the drapes closed, which made it very hot in the room. But for the rest of the night I huddled in bed, fetal position, shivering.

"Any news from the police yet? Have they caught that rat?" Sue asked.

My heart jumped, and my eyes fled to Dad.

"No." With one finger Dad viciously mashed a bread crumb into the table. "But I'll tell you this! If I catch him first, I'll murder him!" Dad's voice shook and his face went red. "I'll tear him apart, limb from limb. And I *will* find him, don't you worry!"

They hadn't caught him! I almost threw up. He'd warned me not to tell. What if he found out, came back. . . .

"You know John Williams in the Motor Vehicle Bureau?" Dad went on, turning to Mom.

"Tom . . ." Mom glanced my way, then touched Dad's arm. "Tom, please. That's no way to talk. Come on now. The police will handle it. Here, have some coffee."

It was like she'd stuck a pin into a balloon. Daddy just kind of slid down in his chair, all deflated. And he didn't even look at me at all.

I couldn't stand to watch him. There was an ache in me so deep, it was beyond tears. I remember when I was about thirteen, and Uncle Joe was visiting. Daddy never liked Mom's brother. He was so—gross. Uncle Joe looked me over and said, "Hey, Andrea's got boobs! No brassiere?" Then he laughed. "Oh, yeah. This generation doesn't go for that." I was mortified. I ran out of the room and locked myself in the bathroom to cry. I could never come out and face my family again.

It was Daddy who came after me. When I finally let him in, he was so gentle. He said a woman should be proud of her breasts, that it was a sign of physical maturity and that they gave beauty to her body.

"How'd it happen?" Sue asked. Her dark eyes were surprisingly sympathetic. She ran a hand nervously through her smooth, short hair.

"I'd like to know, too," Mom said, coming to sit down. "All we've heard so far has been second-hand."

The tears were so close to the surface, and I was feeling so dizzy, so rotten, that talking about it now was the last thing I wanted to do. But they had the right to know. So I began by admitting my error. "I hitched. *We* hitched, from Santa Monica." I brought the hot coffee cup up to my cold cheek, enjoying the burn, like punishment. I looked at my mom. "I know," I said. "You warned me not to. I promised I wouldn't. But I did." My mother put a hand over her mouth, to hide—what? At the time I thought it was pity. Now I wonder if it wasn't anger.

"It was stupid," I went on. "Oh, God, it was stupid! You told me at least a hundred times. If only I'd listened!" The regret was so strong, I couldn't stand it. I put my cup down, lay my head on my crossed arms on the table, and just sobbed.

"Hey, Andrea," Sue said. "I know it must have been awful. But it's not the end of the world. So you made a mistake. We all make mistakes."

Her words were some comfort, but then she added, "Big deal. You're not a virgin anymore. Half the girls at the school aren't."

That made me cry more, because she just didn't understand. It wasn't the virgin thing so much as the *how* of it. I was violated . . . degraded . . . threatened with my life. . . . Didn't she understand?

"I think I'm going to . . ." I jumped up from the table and ran to the sink, holding my hands over my stomach and retching. My mother came up quickly from behind and put her palm on my forehead. I pulled it off. Vomiting is something you have to do completely alone.

When I sat down again, I pushed the coffee away. Even that seemed repulsive now. All I wanted was to get back to bed.

"Well, what do we say?" Sue asked.

"What do you mean?" my mother asked.

"Do we tell anyone? What do I tell my friends?"

"You don't tell them anything! You're going to act as if this never happened. No one must know!"

"Wait a minute, Laura," Daddy said. "Those girls who picked her up know."

"But they promised to keep it secret. I spoke to them. They know how harmful . . ."

"Hah," Sue said. "Karen's in my government class. She doesn't even know the meaning of the word *secret*. I think she knows when a girl gets pregnant before the girl's boyfriend does. Do you think she can keep such delicious news to herself, just because you asked?"

The nausea returned, bringing back a clammy, cold sweat, and the taste in my mouth was awful. Sue's words didn't touch me until after the nausea passed. Only then did I think what it meant, that everyone would know, even Jeffrey's little friends. Every time I'd walk down the street now, I'd wonder what people were thinking. Would the kids at school be picturing me in all those weird poses in *The Joy of Sex?*

Daddy put a hand on mine. "School's a few weeks off yet. By then it will all be forgotten."

"Right," Mom said. "I think Andrea should just put it all out of her head, forget the whole thing. Pretend it never happened."

Sue snorted. "Boy, are you naive! How's she supposed to do that? It did happen, you know! What's more, the police won't let her forget so easily. They'll be after her to check more pictures. Maybe she'll have to go down and identify suspects. If they catch the guy, there'll even be a trial."

"No!" Mom blurted out. She looked scared and her face got red. Then she swallowed and in a deliberate, controlled voice said, "I just don't want that. It's an ugly, dirty thing that happened. Airing it in public would just . . ." She stirred her coffee angrily.

"Now just a minute!" Dad interrupted. "You mean to say, we *shouldn't* press charges? That if they catch that guy, we should just let him go free?"

"Yes!" Mother said defiantly. "Do you want Andrea to have to go through all that again? Can you think what they'd do to her in a courtroom?"

My father frowned, then he said, "I don't think we should get into this now. There's plenty of time for that later. We're not helping Andrea with this kind of talk."

They weren't. All they were doing was making me feel worse. I was still hurting and nauseated. Now, in addition, I was worried about the future and feeling guilty. Not only about what happened to me, because down deep I felt maybe I could have prevented it, but because of what effect it had on them, on the whole family. Dad—and his barely controlled rage. Mom—and her shame about it all. Sue—and her resentment under the thin coat of sympathy. Even Jeffrey who, if he learned what happened, would look at me differently, and have to suffer the jokes and dirty comments of his classmates.

My mother held up a spoon and pointed it at my father. "Well, I'll tell you what I think," she said. "I think Andrea should try to pull herself together as fast as possible. We're not to stew about this with her. It only gets her more upset. No. The faster she gets back to her normal routine, the better. She should go back to work. The sooner the better." She looked at me. "That way, you won't have time to brood."

The phone rang, stopping me from answering

her. I felt a shudder of fear. Would that be the police calling, or David, or the girls? Could the newspapers have learned of it? It stopped ringing before any of us could get to it. A minute later Jeffrey came into the room. Mom stiffened. I could guess why. She would be wondering why he was in the house, and if he had been eavesdropping again.

"Hey," Jeff said, looking us over suspiciously. "How come you're home today, Daddy? And why isn't Sue at work?" Then he looked at me and said, "David's on the phone."

I crossed my arms over my chest and began to shiver. My head kept on shaking No.

"I think you should, Andrea. What will he think?" my mother said.

"Who the hell cares what he thinks? Or what anyone thinks!" my father exploded. "It's Andrea we should be thinking of." He turned to Jeff. "Tell him she's out."

"But she isn't," Jeff said. "Besides, I already told him she's having breakfast."

"Well, *un*tell him. Just say she's gone out. Go on, Jeff. Do as you're told," Dad said.

Jeffrey looked uncertain, then he shrugged and retreated to complete the call in the other room.

"Well," said Mother, letting out a deep sigh. "Now what?"

"I don't know about anyone else, but I'm going to work," Sue said. "I don't see any use in my staying home all day, do you?"

No, certainly not, I thought. If you stayed home,

we wouldn't talk anyway. I couldn't tell you how I really feel, because you always misunderstand, or make light of my feelings, or tell me I'm crazy to feel as I do. I'm just an annoyance to you now anyway. So go.

"May I go back to bed?" I asked.

"Sure, honey," Dad said. "You feeling better? Want some help?"

I got up. It felt like I was on a rolling ship. "I'll be okay," I said. "Just leave me alone."

As I made my way back to my bedroom, I heard their voices drop. Whispering again. Behind my back. About me.

7

If morning sickness is anything like how you feel
from the morning-after pill, then I never want to
become pregnant. Between bouts in the bathroom, where I spewed out my guts, I lay exhausted
in bed, too tired to think.

Now and then a thought would half surface,
like the doctor talking with my parents, asking
permission to give me this pill. Stilbestrol, I think
he called it. You had to take it twice a day for five
days. "It's not something I prescribe lightly," he
said.

Mother jumped on his words sharply. "Why?
Are there dangers?"

"Some twenty years ago we used to prescribe
the drug for women who aborted easily. Now
we're seeing cervical problems in some of their
female offspring." He paused, as if considering
whether he should add anything. "And we've had

some problems with postmenopausal women who were on the drug regularly—unusual bleeding, for example." Hurriedly he added, "But in Andrea's case, considering the trauma she's already been through, I'd say it's called for. After all, you don't want her to face an abortion after all this, too?"

My father started to object.

"Tom," Mother said wearily. "She's two weeks from her period, the most fertile time of the month."

And so it was decided, not by me, the one it would effect, but by *them*. And if I let myself dwell on it, in those moments between upchucking, a cold terror began to creep into me. Would the drug hurt me later? Would it stay in my system and do harm to my children? Were there unknown effects, like cancer? I began to dwell on that, picturing the cancer already growing, spreading through my body, rotting it slowly . . . agonizingly. . . .

"Andrea . . ." Mother came into the room, trying to look cheerful. ". . . here, honey. Sit up. The doctor prescribed something to curb the nausea."

I sat up and reached for the water and the new pill. Mother smoothed a hand over my wet forehead, then went to the window. "It's like an oven in here! Why do you want your windows closed like that?"

"Leave them! It's not too hot! Really! Leave them closed!" I couldn't say that *he* knew I lived off Adlon. What if he asked around, asked my brother's friends, any of the kids who played on the streets each day? All he'd have to do was describe me, and they'd know. He could come back, climb in my bedroom window . . .

"Just a little bit." Mother slid the window open three or four inches. "There. A breeze. You'll feel better." She returned to my bed, sat down, and took my hand in hers. "Kim called. Wanted to know how you were. I told her you weren't ready for company. And Officer Corbett. He wants to come by in an hour, take you for a ride, see if you can identify—where it happened." Mother looked away. "You don't have to, you know."

I nodded.

"I told him you were feeling rotten, and that I'd rather he waited a day or so, but he was pretty insistent. Said they might be able to pick up tire tracks—or other evidence. By tomorrow it could be gone."

"Will he come in a *police* car?" I was thinking of what my mother would worry about—the neighbors.

Mother cleared her throat. "No." Again, she looked away, suddenly very interested in a loose thread on the bedspread. "In his own car. I asked him that."

"Do I have to go along? Will *you* come—or Daddy?"

"Daddy will go, if you want. I just don't think I . . ." She didn't finish the sentence, but smiled a funny, embarrassed smile. She got up. "Anyway, when he comes—if you're still feeling like this, I'll just tell him you're not up to it. Okay?"

"Okay." I watched her go to the door. For a moment she stood there, looking back at me, but not quite into my eyes. "Jeffrey wants to come in. I told him you'd see him for a minute." She put a finger to her lips. "Not a word to him about . . . 'your trouble.' Right?"

I turned my head away, not answering. My chest was bursting again with a need to cry—cry, scream, sob great, heartsick tears. Mommy was shutting me out. She hadn't asked a single question, didn't seem to want to know. Couldn't bring herself to talk about it, couldn't even use the word, it was so revolting to her. It made me feel so alone with it, so isolated, I wanted to die. I wondered what she could be thinking. Would she be wondering if I had brought it on myself, if maybe I could have talked my way out of it, or somehow fought back? Did she think I was dirty now, used, secondhand—the words I was already calling myself in my head—words that screamed at me in red, capital letters?

I got out of bed slowly, so the dizziness wouldn't return, and went to the window to lock it again. When I turned around, Jeffrey was there, staring at me.

Just looking at him made the tears come. I wiped them away angrily, and tried to smile. Jeffrey didn't return my smile. He just came over to me and threw his arms around my waist and hugged me, his head against my chest.

"Hey." I pulled him off. "What's all this?"

"Something's wrong. And nobody will tell me. What's happening, Andrea?"

"Nothing's happening." I kicked some of my stuffed animals out of the way, picked up Frog, and dropped down into the beanbag chair. Jeffrey cleared away some books, and sat cross-legged, opposite me.

"You never lie to me, Andrea. Something *is* happening. Otherwise Daddy and Sue wouldn't be home . . . and they wouldn't be shooing me out of the way all the time. Besides, you're crying."

"I *am not.*" My voice came out high and cracked and hearing it made me laugh and cry at the same time. I clutched Frog tightly and just blubbered, with my face in his head.

Jeffrey didn't seem to know what to make of it. At first he laughed, too, uncertainly, like he thought he'd maybe missed something that was supposed to be funny. But then he frowned and just sat there watching. I couldn't stop myself. I stuffed my fist into my mouth, trying to swallow the noise, because I didn't want them to hear, didn't want my parents to come in. But it was like trying to stop a dam from bursting. I felt so awful, letting him see me that way, that I just kind of crawled out of the chair and staggered over to the bed, and fell face down on the white-eyelet spread.

When it was almost over, Jeffrey shoved a tissue box near my head. I pulled out a batch, blew my nose, wiped my eyes, and then just lay there, exhausted. Then I felt Jeff's finger jab my arm.

"I'm sorry you feel so bad, Andrea. I won't ask any more questions. Honest. You want me to leave?"

"Uh-uh," I mumbled.

He was quiet for a minute, then he said, "Want to play Mastermind?"

"Uh-huh."

"I'll set up."

I could hear him moving things off the ice-cream table I use as a desk, and sorting through the pile of games and junk on the floor near the window. It was comforting, somehow, having him there, hearing him go through the motions of what we did so often together.

"You want to start? I won't look." He covered his eyes with his hands.

I went to the table and, with my right hand, set out the colored pins behind the barrier: two reds, a white, and a black. With my left I held Frog close. "Ready," I said.

Jeff stared hard at the barrier as if he were trying to see through it. Then he reached in the box and took out four colored pins which he set in the holes of the first row. He had one color, the red, in the right position. I showed him that, by putting a black pin on the side. Maybe it was having my mind on something else, or maybe it was the pill for nausea, but I began to feel better.

"Your warts look smaller," I said. "Doesn't look like thirty-seven to me."

"There are though." Jeff held up the backs of

his hands. "Look. Aren't they ugly? There's a kid on Adlon says I probably got them from toads. Remember last summer when I found all those toads up at Mammoth?"

"I remember. But that's just an old wives' tale."

"You know what else this kid said? He told me if I licked each wart once a day at midnight, they'd disappear. You think it might work?"

"How about the potato cure?"

"I tried that for a month, don't you remember? I rubbed the juice over them every night, just like the man said. But it didn't do any good."

"Bring your hands close. Maybe Frog can help. You know how the princess kissed the frog and turned him into a prince? Well, maybe if Frog kissed the warts, he'd turn them into . . ."

"You know that's silly. You're making fun of me." He sat on his hands.

"It's not silly if you believe in it."

"Well, I don't. I hate them. I feel so—ugly."

"Oh, Jeff," I said. "You're not ugly. Maybe your hands are, but it's what's inside you that counts."

For a while we just looked at each other with that kind of special feeling we seem to have for each other. Then Jeff's face grew serious. "Why were you at the police station, Andrea? Did you do something wrong?"

"No," I said.

"You can tell me. Did you shoplift? I heard a lot of kids at school were doing things like that."

"Do you really think *I'd* do that?"

"No. But . . . if you did . . . maybe just once, you know . . . I swiped some bubble gum at the Variety Store once. Boy, it was scary. I figure if *I* could do that . . . maybe you . . ." He took some new pins from the box and began to place them on the board.

"I didn't shoplift," I said. "And you shouldn't either." I knew then I had to tell him something. It wasn't fair to keep him wondering, being swept aside each time the family gathered as if he wasn't part of us. "I was hurt badly . . . by a man."

He looked up, and his eyes went dark. "I don't understand. You mean he hit you? Did you know him?"

"No, I don't know him, and I don't know why. But he hurt me badly, and the police are trying to find him."

"But how did it happen? Where were you? Did he make those scratches on your face? Is that why you're taking pills?"

I could feel the misery welling up inside again. For the few minutes we'd been playing the game, it had lain submerged. "Please, Jeff," I pleaded. "Don't ask any more questions. Just—let's play."

The new pill must have worked, because by the time Officer Corbett arrived, I was feeling almost normal. At least the nausea was gone. The rest of me felt far away someplace, like I was seeing everything through thick panes of dirty glass.

"I'm coming with you," my father announced when Corbett greeted me.

"I'd rather you didn't, sir," Corbett said. "Andrea may find it harder."

My father looked at me, but I tried not to show how much I wanted him to come. Somehow, the decision had to be his, not because I'd asked Mom.

"I'm coming, nevertheless," Dad said. He went to the door and opened it for us, then followed us out to Corbett's car.

Corbett began at the place where the girls had picked me up. From there, we drove up Hayvenhurst, and down the first streets that I remembered. After that it became confused. But Corbett must have known the geography of the area pretty well, because whenever I wasn't sure, he always seemed to get us on a street which would lead up into the more remote parts of the hills.

We didn't talk much. I just sat with my hands clenched tight against my stomach, leaning forward in the front seat, and watching the houses go by. Every now and then something—a bottle-brush bush, or a white oleander—or a special garden would look familiar, and my heart would lurch, like when you have a test sprung on you suddenly.

All the time we drove, Dad sat in the back, silent. I forgot he was even there. It wasn't until we were on the final stretch of road—and I knew it was—that I became conscious of him. He was leaning forward, gripping the top of the front seat with his hands as tightly sprung as I was. I see him that way now, but at the time I was so locked

into my own feelings, so close to the terror of the
day before, that I only glanced at him, storing
what I saw to take out and look at later.

"Is this it?" Corbett asked, pulling off the road
toward the eucalyptus grove.

"Yes." There it was, the place where he'd parked,
the rocks, the weeds, the bushes he'd dragged me
through, all so innocent-looking now, like a place
to go on a picnic. Maybe it never happened. Maybe
it was only a bad dream after all. But my body
told me otherwise. Every muscle, every nerve,
every cell knew. Perspiration gushed, hot then
cold, from every pore. My legs dug into the floor
like they were screwed there.

Corbett parked and got out while I just stayed
put, fists jammed tightly against my lips, eyes
glued to the dashboard. He came around to my
side of the car and opened the door.

"I hate asking you to go through this, but can
you show me precisely? Then you can go back to
the car if you like." Daddy got out, prepared to
come along, but Corbett stopped him. "I'll be looking for footprints," he said. "Don't want to get
confused by another set. When I'm done, if you
like, you can take a look, but I don't see what good
it would do."

Corbett carried a camera and a pad and followed me. As soon as I reached the spot, I pointed
and started back. I didn't want to wait there and
relive it. Yet to my eye, in that brief look, there
was nothing on the ground out of order. The rocks
which had bruised my back could have been rocks

anywhere. No bushes seemed to be broken or trampled. As far as I could see, there was no sign I had ever been there before.

From the car I could see Corbett taking pictures and writing on the pad. Daddy stood beside the car watching, too, not talking. I tried not to think, tried to just concentrate on what Corbett was doing. But it didn't always work. Flashes of *him* sizzled alive, shrieking his anger because he couldn't perform, blaming me . . . I couldn't help it. Tears slid down my cheeks and vomit swam in my mouth.

After a while Corbett came back and Daddy took off. Poor Dad. Now I realize he must have been looking for some clue Corbett missed, something that might lead him to my attacker.

I was sitting in the front seat, eyes closed, arms crossed when Daddy left. Corbett came to stand outside the car beside me. He leaned against the door and wrote on the pad or looked toward my Dad. "How's it going?"

"Okay, I guess," I said.

"Pretty tough at home? Your father seems real uptight. What about your mother?"

"She's okay."

He didn't say anything for a second then said, "Not so. She scooted out of the living room as fast as she could when I came in. Like I had the plague or something. She treating you the same way?"

I didn't answer.

"Thought so." He walked away from the car

and bent down to look at something. Then he took a picture and came back. "You oughta talk about it. Write it down or something. Don't bottle it up, you know. That's bad."

I didn't say anything to that, either, because his words were hurting me, bringing on the dumb tears again.

"Your dad's coming back," he said. "So I'll tell you this quick. We have a Rape Hotline in town. I'll give you the number. Call them. Talk it out. You'll feel better. Will you promise?"

"My mother wouldn't like that." I stared down at my hands.

"Don't tell her." Corbett's voice was low. Then in a hearty tone he said, "Well, Mr. Cranston, find anything?"

Daddy got into the car and slammed the door. "Nothing," he grumbled.

8

By Saturday there was no doubt in my mind that I had to get back to work. Except for the few hours with Corbett on Thursday I spent most of the time indoors in my room. And there, alone, it was hard not to think.

Mom was like a hummingbird, buzzing around me, then darting off brightly to run this or that errand. Not that she neglected me—she gave me lemonade by the gallon, she brought me a pile of books from the library, and even broke the cardinal rule that there's no TV on till 9 P.M. when she asked if I'd like to watch. But not once did she really sit down, look at me, and talk.

It wasn't that I wanted to rehash the same awful experience again; I did that often enough in my head. What I hurt so badly for was to hear her say, "Andrea, you're the same good person, the same lovely daughter you were before. I don't love you any less. And when you feel bad, remember: I'm always here, always ready to listen."

But she didn't. She wanted everything to be normal again, didn't want to think I hurt. Knowing that was how she wanted it, I tried my best to *act* normal. For instance one morning Mom dropped a plastic margarine dish, with a new square of margarine, on the kitchen floor. Normally that would have rated a "whoops" and a giggle. Instead, she scooped up the yellow glop and cursed her clumsiness in a burst of self-hate. I just stood there holding in my tears, keeping my face that nice bland blankness that was becoming second nature, and saying nothing.

My father, in his way, was no better than Mom. It was as if he had a big black cloud over him. He sat at supper preoccupied, and he'd bark at Jeff or Mom, though he was gentle with me. At night, from their bedroom, I could hear arguments going on between Mom and him till late.

Jeff was an angel. He'd come in and want to play a game, or tell me about the Williams's pups and want me to go see them, but it was no substitute for real gut-level talking.

Which leaves Sue. She was at work all day, but there were evenings. And I think she did try to get through to me.

Like Friday night. Right after dinner, I excused myself. The effort to keep up bright conversation had become too much, and I went to my room to read. But my room didn't seem safe any longer. Though the light was on and the curtains were closed, I felt visible. I was beginning to listen to even the slightest sound outside. I'd read a sentence then have to read it again, and it still didn't mean anything because my mind wasn't on it. I'd hear a scratching sound and wonder if it was him, trying to unlatch the gate to the side yard. Or a sighing sound, and think maybe it was *him*. Then, when the dog next door began barking, I took it to mean only one thing: Someone strange was near her territory.

After a while I couldn't stand it anymore. If he was after me again, I had to know. I just had to find out, had to face it, so I turned off the light and went to the window. Then, standing in the dark, forcing myself to wait till my eyes adjusted, I parted the curtain a little and looked out.

There was still enough moonlight to see much of the side yard, but not enough to explain all the shadows. Still I was sure someone was out there. On the other side of the elm tree, between it and the pyracantha bushes.

I was standing there with my fist to my mouth, shaking, when Sue came in. She switched on the light, saw me there, and came immediately to my side.

"What is it?" she whispered.

"He's out there."

"That's crazy. He couldn't be." She put her arm

around me. "Come on. You're just nervous. Sit down, we'll talk."

"No," I said, resisting her pull. "He *is* there. Turn off the light. You'll see!"

Sue went immediately to the light switch and turned it off, then returned to look with me at the yard.

"Where?"

I told her where to look.

"You need glasses. That's no man, it's just part of the bush," she said.

God, how I wanted to believe her, but my eyes didn't trust what she said. And my head was already reasoning that in the time the light was on, he'd slipped away.

"Look . . . I'm telling you, it's only a bush. I'll prove it. Come outside."

"No!"

"Okay," she said. "Then you stay here, and I'll go out and you can watch."

I didn't object, and she turned quickly and left the room, leaving me still in the dark, watching the yard. Presently, there she was, waving to me. Then she walked directly to the bush I suspected and shook her head. Not only that, she systematically explored as much of the yard as was within my view, coming back to my window, shaking her head and shrugging to show me there was nothing out there. It may have been that there was no one there then. But there had been *before*. I was sure of it.

When she came back in, I had turned my bedside lamp on and was sitting on my bed with my arms around my legs and my head on my knees. She sat down beside me.

"You're getting paranoid, Andrea—thinking he's still after you. He'd be crazy, coming here— even if he knew where you lived. He must know you might have told the police, and that they might even be watching the house to protect you."

"But they're not."

"Still, he might *think* that."

"He said he'd kill me if I told."

"That was just to scare you." She studied me for a time, then said, "Mom has some Valium. Want me to ask for one?"

"No!" A tranquilizer might put me to sleep, knock me out so hard I couldn't hear when he came—because, no matter what anyone said, I was sure he would come.

"Then if you don't want a tranquilizer, maybe you better stop squirreling yourself away like this in the dark. Go in with the family. Go back to work again, like Mom says. Try to pick up where you left off." Her voice dropped. "It's the only way to forget.

"David's called twice. Have you returned his call?" she asked.

"No." I picked up Frog and ran my fingers over his bristly plush.

"Why not?"

"I just couldn't. I don't want to see boys now . . . not yet."

"But David? I thought he was special."

"No. I wouldn't want him to—touch me." I turned my head away. My stomach was beginning to churn.

"So . . . tell him."

"Tell him what happened? I couldn't."

"It was his fault, really. He should never have let you go home alone. If he wasn't so damned concerned for earning a buck."

Typical Sue. Ever since Paul, her first love, had dropped her, she didn't really seem to like guys, even though she went out a lot.

"It wasn't his fault. I shamed him, told him he was acting like Mom."

"I don't care. He shouldn't have let you get back in that car!"

I shrugged. Who knows? Maybe she was right. But what difference did it make now? Besides, Corbett had said it might have happened, even with David along. Maybe even worse. When I told Sue that, she said, "Worse? How could it have been worse?"

I looked her straight in the eye and said, "Neither of us would be here today."

I think that got to her, because her eyes opened wide and her hand flew to her mouth. I think she would have embraced me if I wasn't sitting in that awkward, fetal position. Instead she put a hand on my arm, shuddered a little, and said, "Let's go watch TV. There's a Woody Allen movie on Channel Nine. Maybe you can put it out of your head, at least for a while."

* * *

I went to work Saturday. While I dressed, my mother kept asking if I was sure, did I really feel ready to face the world again. "I'm sure," I said, giving her one of my fake "everything's okay" looks. "Well, then," she said. "I'll drive you and pick you up after work." A barely suppressed excitement told me what I already knew—she could hardly wait for me to be gone so she could pretend everything was normal again.

"You can't be driving me every day. It would take too much of your time," I said, watching her closely.

"Still, you'd probably feel better, wouldn't you, not having to take the bus?"

I could see she was wavering. And something obstinate in me wanted to test her, wanted to see how far I had to push before she'd agree that I could go alone. By making her agree with me, I'd push myself. God, how complicated people are. All the time I wanted to scream, "Mommy, *please* drive me! Stay near me every minute of the day." But I just couldn't. I was trying to read how she felt in every word, movement, and inflection of her voice so I could give her what she wanted. And every sign I read said, "Andrea, I'm uncomfortable with you now. I'm ashamed of myself for feeling like this, but I can't help it. Tell me you're okay, that you're holding up, that this hasn't scarred you permanently, and *I'll believe you.*"

So I said, "There'll be a hundred people on the bus. Besides, if you're really worried, I'll get a seat near the driver."

"But if it's crowded?"

"It won't be. It's Saturday. Besides, I could stand near the driver if it is."

"I suppose," she said thoughtfully. "But I don't want you walking that mile to the bus stop. The least I can do is drive you there." I saw the worry lines crease her forehead again. "But what about when you get to Westwood? You still have a block or so to walk."

Corbett's story about the girl who was pulled into the van in broad daylight flickered through my mind, but I smothered it quickly.

"You know what the streets are like in Westwood, Mom. Full of middle-class browsers and students. Perfectly safe. Besides," I added, knowing this was just what she wanted to hear most, "I've got to face it sometime. It may as well be now."

And so, by 8:45 I was safely delivered to the corner of Ventura Boulevard and Hayvenhurst to await the Westwood bus. Concerned mother sat in the car at the Arco Station, watching until the bus actually stopped and I stepped on.

It was weird, being on my own again. Before, when I'd take the bus to Westwood, I'd drop my change into the box and plop down on the nearest seat, never thinking who sat next to me. I'd read or talk to my seatmate or study the people in the bus and wonder what kind of lives they led. It would all be kind of an adventure. It was as if I was covered with antennas, and they were all receiving good vibes.

But this time it was totally different. As soon as the bus doors slammed, I got this frantic, closed-in feeling. The bus driver seemed to be looking at me differently, as if he knew. The seated passengers watched me, too, and for a terrified moment, I stood in the aisle, feeling naked and exposed. Where was it safe to sit? Near the old man? Next to the lady with the baby? Near the two girls dressed for a day at the beach? No. They might talk to me, ask questions. I nearly fell into a seat on the aisle, leaving the window seat empty. In some remote part of my brain I must have figured that most people wouldn't bother climbing over someone else to take a window seat, choice though it was, unless the bus was full. Besides, an aisle seat gave me freedom to jump up quickly.

As the bus moved off, I sat rigid, hands tightly clasped in my lap. When passengers came on, I kept my eyes deliberately averted, not wanting to invite a seatmate by any show of openness. And though my eyes were fixed on the window, they saw nothing, because every nerve, every sense, all my antennas—were tuned elsewhere—to the threats of those around me—coming on or going off the bus.

I had read a book recently, called *Dune*. It was about a future society in which there were women who practiced mental, physical, and genetic control. One of the ways they dealt with fear was to repeat a litany against it. I think it went something like this: *Fear is the mind-killer. I must not fear. I will face my fear. And where it has been, there will be nothing, only me.*

On the bus that day, I started repeating that litany. It helped. It kept my mind too busy for anything else to be there.

It's about a two-block walk from the bus stop in Westwood to 31 Flavors. All the way to the shop, I repeated my litany. Pier 1 Imports might have changed their window display, but I wouldn't have known. The fragrance of coffee and fresh donuts, or of Lum's beer-brewed hot dogs—normally sharp to my nose and taste buds—were missing that day. For all my powers were concentrated on one thing, getting safely to my job, moving my feet forward one after the other down the street as my mind repeated over and over, Fear is the mind-killer . . . I must not fear . . .

9

My mother was right about one thing. Work is good for getting your mind off your troubles. At least for a while. From the minute I set foot inside the ice cream store and put on my apron, I performed like a programmed robot. Sweep the floor. Windex the glass cases. Refill the nuts- and chocolate syrup- and cherry- and whipped-cream dispensers. Replace the empty five-gallon ice cream containers. No time for the mind to wander. No time to feel.

"Double scoop? Sundae? Pistachio and Mandarin Orange? Banana split? What flavor syrup? That will be ninety-six cents, thirty-five cents, a dollar thirty-five . . ."

About one o'clock, when the traffic in the store was heaviest and there were three of us behind the counter working nonstop, I looked up to see Karen and Cindy—the girl who drove the car that picked me up—staring at me.

"Hi!" My hands went icy. "Number seventy-nine?" I looked around, hoping they weren't holding that number. Nobody came to the counter. "Eighty?"

"That's us," Cindy said, smiling brightly. She leaned on the glass counter and lowered her voice. "How's it going?"

"Fine. What'll you have?"

"Your mother said you didn't want to speak to anyone, but when we called today, she said you'd gone back to work."

I could feel Bob's eyes on me. He's the store manager, and he frowns on friends dropping by just to chat. He always manages to amble over to where he can watch and hear so you cut it short. "What'll it be?" I asked again.

"I'll have a double scoop of Cherry Vanilla," Karen said.

Cindy smiled at Bob. "Give me a . . . let's see . . ." She walked along the counter, checking out the different flavors, but every few seconds, looked back to see if Bob was still watching. "What's the flavor of the month?"

"Peach Daiquiri." My heart was racing, and I wanted to run into the back room until they left. Instead, I started scooping from a new container of awfully hard Cherry Vanilla.

Bob left to serve someone at the frozen-pie

counter, and immediately, Cindy was back. "You get a lunch break? We'll wait for you at Lum's. How soon you think you can get off?"

"I don't get a break. Not till three o'clock." I handed the cone to Karen. "What do you want, Cindy?"

"We just wanted to see you, see how you were," Cindy said. "Did they catch the guy? What are the police doing?" She gave me a self-conscious smile. "You never told us . . . *what* he did."

People were hearing her, watching me. Carol, working next to me, darted a surprised look my way. "Cindy . . . do you want any ice cream or not?" My throat began to hurt.

"Just one scoop Rocky Road. So? We'll wait till three for you. Lum's. Okay?"

"That'll be one dollar and five cents." I handed the napkin-wrapped cone to Cindy and waited for her to give me the money, avoiding her eyes, watching her hands instead as she fumbled in her purse. But she wouldn't let me escape. She held out two dollars, then wouldn't release them until I looked at her. "Will you come?"

I wanted to say, What for? What do you want from me? Is it to help, or is it just to pry? Cindy had never shown the slightest interest in me at school, and Karen, like Sue said, was the school gossip. "I don't know. We may be busy, and I won't be able to get away."

"That's okay. We'll wait." Cindy let go of the money at last, but her eyes never left me as her

tongue licked around the scoop of ice cream.
Then, raising the cone in farewell, she nodded at
Karen and called over her shoulder, "See you at
three."

The closer it got to three o'clock, the clumsier
I became. Ice cream didn't stick on the cones.
Cones crumpled. Cherries dropped from the
spoons because my hand wouldn't hold steady.
I began bumping into the other people behind the
counter. Something about the girls' manner
seemed not quite honest. In the car they'd been
genuinely concerned, but in the shop there was a
breathless anticipation to them, like they could
hardly wait to hear all the ugly, dirty details.

Bob finally came up to me and asked if I was
feeling okay. Was I not over the virus my mother
had called in about Thursday and Friday?

"Guess I'm still a little shaky," I said. "Could I
take an early break?"

"Carol?" Bob asked. "Want to trade breaks with
Andrea?"

Carol agreed readily, and I fled to the back
room.

Now what to do? I asked myself.

It was a little past two. I hadn't had my lunch,
but food didn't matter. What really did matter
was that somehow, I needed to outwit the three
o'clock deadline. Even if I did nothing except sit
in the back room for the next half hour and stare
at the walls, when three came, I didn't have to
go out there and face the girls. They could come

back and ask me when I would get my break, and I could honestly say I wouldn't be free till six-thirty, when it was time to go home.

So what to do now? If I left the shop to get a bite at the donut place or McDonald's, there was the danger I'd run into the girls, because they wouldn't head for Lum's until close to three. Then I'd stay here. Where no one would bother me. In the bathroom.

I went into the tiny bathroom in the back and locked the door. I pulled the toilet lid down and sat down to stare at the cracked tile floor and think.

It was the first time, really, that I could examine all the things that had been happening to me. At home in my room I felt like a prisoner of my parents' wills. I was not to *think* about what happened. Now, away from home, those restrictions didn't apply.

First, *him*. I let myself relive for an instant those first awful moments, the look of hate on his face, his cruel hands, the way he kept on trying and blamed me when he couldn't. It was again like a knife cutting my heart up in little shreds. I felt as if I was joined to that stranger by an invisible chain. No matter which way I turned, how I twisted or tried to break free, I couldn't. He would always be there at the other end. I could almost see him, now, nearby perhaps, walking the very streets of Westwood, looking for me. *Had David and I spoken of my job here?* For a frantic moment I searched my memory, trying to recall every tidbit of conversation in that car. But no. Where I worked, or that I even worked at all, had never come up.

What was I going to do? I just couldn't go on like this, carrying this burden inside me, unable to share its weight. Corbett had suggested calling someone. I had the phone number in my purse. But my mind went from that to Corbett himself, and to wondering why he had been so interested— now that I had time to examine it—in the *precise details* of the attack. Was he like the girls—just "curious"? What possible purpose was there for him to know *everything*? The car's description, the man's description—these things I could under-stand. *But the rest?*

"Andrea, Andrea?" Someone was knocking on the door. "You in there?"

I got up and unlocked the bathroom door. Carol was standing outside. Carol is Japanese. Slight and pretty, a quiet girl whom you don't get to know quickly. She's a psych major at UCLA and works part-time at two jobs during the summer.

"You okay?" she asked with concern. I knew she wouldn't press me further, even though she must have been curious, having heard Cindy's re-marks about the police.

I turned to wash my hands in the small sink. "I'm sorry. Did I overstay my break? I'll be right in." I combed my hair quickly and started for the front of the shop.

"No . . . that's not it. You have a phone call. Someone named David."

I had told David never to call me at work. Bob didn't like the employees to take personal calls. And I didn't really feel ready to talk to him anyway. What would I say? And how would I feel? Everything was different now and until I sorted it out, David would have to wait.

"Bob took the call," Carol said. "Better hurry."

In the time I'd been in the back, business had picked up again, and the other employees were scurrying this way and that, making milk shakes and splits and filling cone orders.

I was conscious of Bob nearby as I picked up the phone, aware that I shouldn't be talking at all, but since I was, that I'd better keep it short.

"Andrea, it's me," David said. "I've been trying to reach you for days. What's going on? Why don't you ever call me back?

"I've just been—busy, David."

"I don't buy that. Are you angry with me? Did I do something wrong? I've only got another two weeks before I leave for school. Everything was so great between us. What's the matter?"

"I can't talk now. You know I'm at work."

"Well, then we'll talk tonight. I'll pick you up after work. I'll break away early. We'll have dinner. Someplace nice for a change. Okay?"

"My mother is coming to pick me up."

"How come? I thought it was a standing date —Saturday nights."

I pressed some ground walnuts into the counter with my finger and turned my back on Bob. Suddenly, hearing David's voice, I *did* want to see him. I wanted to pour out everything to him. It didn't occur to me how he might take it—only that I needed to talk. "Okay . . ." I mumbled.

"Huh? Did you say okay?" David's voice had brightened.

"Yes."

"Wonderful. Listen, I'll save you a call to your mother. I'll phone her. *Hey*, Andy . . . I'm so glad! See you at six-thirty?"

"Okay." I hung up, and for the first time all day, felt good. Bob looked me over and smiled. "Feeling better?"

"Lots." I glanced up at the number board and pressed the button. "Thirty-six?"

Karen came in about 3:20. She tried to catch my eye from behind a group of noisy birthday kids. For a while I pretended not to notice, then just shrugged in a hopeless way and threw out my hands as if to say: "What can I do? You can see how busy we are." She stood around for a while longer, but when I ignored her, she finally left—to tell Cindy, I would guess—that their fun afternoon poking into Andrea's sex life would have to be postponed.

David came in just before 6:30. He was carrying a large, flat package wrapped in brown paper, and wearing a self-satisfied grin on his face. He took a seat and watched as I served my last cus-

tomer, a woman who couldn't make up her mind
about the flavor. "It's always so hard to decide,"
she complained.

David jumped up, came to the counter, and
pretended great interest in the display case. "Yum,
nothing like Jamoca Almond Fudge," he said.

"Yes, that's a good idea. I'll have a scoop of
that—what the young man just said—Jamoca
Almond Fudge," the lady said at last.

"Single or double?" David asked.

"Double."

David grinned at me, but I couldn't return his
smile. Part of me had pulled inward, like a turtle
retreating into its shell. Now that he was here, in
front of me, I was scared. It was only three days
since we'd seen each other. For him, nothing had
changed, while for me—everything had. One instant I let myself feel toward him as I had; in the
next, I held him off, making him seem an unwel-
come stranger. I didn't know now how I'd tell
him, or even if I could. And if I did tell him, I
didn't know how he'd take it.

"Hey," he said, taking my arm when I came out.
"We're going to the Rathskeller for dinner. And I
have a surprise. A present." He held out the package to show me. "Guess."

I tried to respond to his joyful mood. "A
record?"

"Oh, come on. Where's your imagination?" He
put an arm around my waist. Usually I love walking that way, falling in step with him like a good
dancer. Instead I changed my gait so it became

awkward and soon he was just holding my hand.

"A pizza?"

"Heck no. I'm no cheapskate. We're going to the Rathskeller to eat, didn't you hear?"

"A portrait of the Fuller Brush Man of the Year?" I asked, trying hard to be funny.

David chuckled. "Warm. Pretty warm. But you don't get to see it till after dinner. Now, tell me why you weren't answering my calls. What happened? Robert Redford giving me competition?"

"Oh, David!" It was so far from the real reason, I nearly burst into tears. All this time he'd been worrying that I'd found somebody else! I'd always thought David was so self-assured, but how fragile even his ego was.

"Hey, what's wrong, Andy?" He stopped in the middle of the street and faced me. Putting his hands on my shoulders, he tried to get me to look at him. But I just shook my head and bit my lip and then put my forehead against his chest. "Did you miss lunch again?" David's voice was gruff. Once before, when I'd missed lunch, I'd been grumpy when he picked me up.

I shook my head against his chest.

He pulled me close, but I stood in the circle of his arms as stiffly as a wooden soldier. At some point, I'd *have* to tell him. "Come on," he said then. "Let's go eat. It's elementary, my dear Watson. You're just hungry. Besides, mother always says, 'the way to a woman's heart is through her stomach.' " He took my arm and steered us down the block again.

10

The Rathskeller's not much to look at from the outside, and as soon as you step inside, it's so dark, it takes your eyes a while to adjust. But once you enter the big room, it's like being transported to the dining hall of a baronial manor. There's a big bar against one wall and a faint smell of beer. And there's a fireplace in the middle of the room which has a fire in it during cold weather. The tables are heavy, polished oak, and the chairs are either tub-shaped or tall-backed like in a castle. The ceilings are high, and the walls have wine bottles encased in rings, like in a wine cellar. Not that I've ever been in one.

Studying the menu gave me an excuse not to talk, but it didn't stop David. He couldn't make up his mind between the Swissburger and the Hawaiianburger and asked playfully would I mind, after

all, if he ordered the onionburger. I felt a cold
sweat suddenly at the implication. Ordinarily I
would have laughed and said, "Go ahead. I'll split
it with you. Then you'll get a *taste* of your own
medicine." But tonight I just hid my face behind
the menu and said, "Whatever you like."

When the waitress came, he pleaded with her
to hurry our order. "This poor child is starved,"
he said. "She hasn't smiled since breakfast."

Finally, orders taken and menus put down,
there was nothing left to make small talk about.
There I was, and there David was watching me,
waiting for me to say something. I picked at a
cuticle and avoided his eyes.

"I do believe your mother is beginning to like
me," David said after a time. "You know how she's
been about our seeing so much of each other
lately. Half the time I'm not even sure if she's
going to give you my messages. But tonight when
I called to tell her I'd bring you home—I could
have sworn she nearly jumped for joy. What do
you suppose got into her?"

The news surprised me, too. And then the prob-
able reason came to me, and with it such a sense
of shame for the way she was using David, that I
wanted to get up and run out of the restaurant
and never see him again.

By my mother's reasoning, David was now the
lesser of two evils. Before, she hassled me end-
lessly that we mustn't become too close—"have
sex"—though she didn't like to use such crude

words. Now she had the opposite worry, that this *experience* of mine would make me hate men. I could just hear her saying, "When you fall off a horse, it's best to get right back on and ride again."

Well, what happened to me wasn't as simple as that. And I wasn't going to let David be used that way!

"Hey, where ya been?" David asked, reaching across the table and putting his hand over my fists. "I've been watching you for five minutes and you're way off some place. What is it, Andy? It's more than just being hungry, isn't it?"

Where I was, was in my head. I pictured telling him. He'd be polite and kind, but end the evening as fast as he could. And never call again. Or he'd be polite and kind, but the next time he called he'd figure, what the heck, she's not a virgin anymore, so what's the difference?

I played with the idea that I wouldn't tell him. But if I didn't, I couldn't go on seeing him without feeling dishonest. In fact I couldn't even be myself anymore, with him not knowing. And what if the girls told? If they talked around (and I was beginning to realize how likely that was), it would be awful—David finding out that way.

"Well, now," the waitress said, before I could decide what to say. "One onionburger with German potato salad and one Hawaiianburger with barbecued beans." She set our plates down. "Two Cokes coming up."

Though he had withdrawn his hand from mine,

David didn't touch his food. He continued to watch me, waiting for an answer.

I shrugged and tried to smile and said, "Your burger's getting cold."

"All right." He concentrated on cutting his onionburger in half. "If you don't want to tell me, we can talk about other things." He looked up. "While I was pounding the pavement today, going door to door with my trusty Fuller Brush kit in my hand and half the dogs in Los Angeles at my heels, I thought about what you said at the beach Wednesday." He reached over to my plate and cut my burger in half. "Time to trade." He took the smaller cut from my plate and pushed his plate over so I could take half of the onionburger.

"Anyhow, I thought, maybe you were right, about people I mean. And you know what? I don't know if my attitude had anything to do with it or not, but the whole day I didn't bump into one nasty person."

My hands began trembling and I hid them on my lap.

"Eat," David said. "Your burger's getting cold." He gave me a quick grin and dug his fork into the potato salad. "That's why I brought you the present."

I picked up my burger and took a half-hearted bite. "Why a present?" I asked with my mouth full. "What's the occasion? Anyway, you shouldn't have. You need that money for college."

"A guy's got a right to do something out of character, now and then." David picked up the package on the seat beside him. "I couldn't resist this. As soon as I saw it, I thought of you." Even in the dim light I recognized that look of tenderness he sometimes had when he said good night. Impulsively he thrust the package across the table at me. "Here, I can hardly wait to see what you think."

I put down my burger and wiped my hands on the napkin. Then, taking the package from him, I turned it over a couple of times, trying to guess what was inside.

"It's not really that much." David seemed suddenly shy and embarrassed, but I could tell he was dying to have me like it. "Go on, open it."

I pushed my plate away and drew my chair back from the table so there was room to lean the package on the table. Then, slipping my finger under the tape, I began to remove the wrapping.

"What is it? It feels like a board." I looked across the table at him.

David leaned eagerly toward me, watching my every move. "What is a board that isn't a board?"

"Riddles, riddles. You're impossible!" I removed the last paper and found myself looking at a brown fiberboard. Puzzled, I held it up, then turned it over.

It was a picture. As I brought it close to the table lantern so I could see it better, my chest felt as if it would burst.

It was a painting of three little girls, arms around each other, skipping across a field. The children were rosy-cheeked, innocent, joyous, almost bursting with a look of pleasure at being free to bound across those green, flower-covered fields.

David jumped up and came to stand behind me so he could look down at the painting from the same viewpoint as I. "See," he said, pointing to the middle child. "The tallest one. That's you. Don't you see that look around the eyes and mouth?"

"Oh, David," I cried, the words sounding strangled to my ears. Tears began sliding down my cheek. David, behind my chair, didn't notice. But then, these deep, awful sounds started coming from inside me. Even though we were at a table in the corner and I tried so hard to disguise it, clearing my throat and all, it didn't help. I was so embarrassed, I just thrust the painting out at David, grabbed my purse, and with one hand over my eyes so no one would see me, I rushed off to the rest room.

When I came back fifteen minutes later, David was seated in a new position at the table, anxiously watching the doorway to the rest rooms. He hadn't eaten much of his dinner, and was nervously turning a salt shaker around and around.

I slipped into my seat and whispered, "I'm sorry." It seemed as if everyone in the restaurant must be watching.

"Do you want to leave? I've paid the bill," David said.

I gestured to the unfinished food. "It's really so good. Why don't you finish? I'm not very hungry."

"That's okay." David got up, tucked the rewrapped painting under his arm, and pulled my chair out. "Maybe you'll want something later."

When we got outside, David didn't say anything, but we just walked, not even holding hands until we got to his car. He unlocked the car door on my side and I got in. Usually I reach over and unlock his door so he won't have to bother with keys, but I guess I just wasn't thinking about things like that, because I settled into the front seat, hands folded, and just waited.

David got in, tossed the painting in the back, then turned to me. "Okay, Andrea. What's it all about? Do you want to talk, or do you want me to take you home?"

"I want to talk," I mumbled, twisting the Navaho rings on my right hand round and round. But then, instead of talking, I stared out the window at the couples strolling by, visible for just a short time under the streetlights, then fading away into the darkness.

"Remember last Wednesday," I began at last, "when we got back to Encino? Remember how you didn't want me to go on alone in the car with that man?"

I didn't look at David through the whole telling, though I could feel his tension, could sense his growing horror. I just sat there in the darkness, twisting my rings and telling my story in this matter-of-fact voice like I was relating the plot of an endless, dull book I had read once, long ago.

When I got to the awful part, David leaned his head on his arms over the steering wheel and started to cry. "Oh, God," he whispered, his shoulders shaking. I couldn't stand to hear him cry, and put a hand on his arm. "David, don't . . ." I felt this deep, sad pain inside. "Please, don't."

He turned his face toward me, all wet with tears, and cried, "It's all my fault! All mine! I should never have listened to you!"

"No, no, it wasn't. The police officer said it could have happened even if you'd been along."

"All that time. Oh, God . . . *all that time* . . . while you . . . !" He shook his head, and the contempt in his voice was thick with self-hate. "All the while that you . . ." He cleared his throat again and again . . . "I was . . . *selling* dumb brushes! What would it have meant—taking another half hour off!"

"Stop it!" I cried. "Don't blame yourself. It wasn't your fault!" The stricken look on his face was so awful that I put my hand to his face.

"Oh, Andrea! I'm so sorry . . . !" He gathered me into his arms, and we held on to each other, crying like two lost children for I don't know how long.

After that we sat close, hand in hand, and I told David the rest of the story, from the time the girls picked me up, through the trip with Corbett and my dad to the place where he'd taken me; even about how Mom, Dad, Sue, and Jeff had reacted. David listened quietly, wiping his eyes from time to time, and asking me a question now and then.

It was so good to be able to tell him everything, to feel his understanding and sympathy, not even slightly tinged with disgust or blame. Because of that, I felt I could ask him what he thought about some of the things that worried me. Like Corbett's prying questions.

"Maybe," David said, softly into the darkness, "it's to get an M.O."

"What's that?"

"Well, when they put out the description of a man on the police radio, his M.O., his *modus operandi*—you know, how he operates—is part of it. Sometimes they can identify a guy just because he always works the same way. Like maybe he only picks up hitchers, or always threatens with a knife, instead of say—a gun."

"Oh," I said. "Is *that* why!" And then I thought of the things he had done to me, things I'd told Corbett but couldn't tell David, and I shivered. How terrible to think *that* kind of information might go out on a police radio! But it made me feel better, too, in a way. Maybe it would help catch the man. And at least Corbett hadn't asked those questions just out of curiosity.

"I want to explain about the picture, why it upset me so," I said then, trying to see David's face in the faint street light.

"You don't have to explain."

"But I do. I really love the painting. It's not that. It's that, you see . . . what you said, about how I looked . . . about the innocence." My throat got all closed up again.

David didn't answer for a minute, but then he said, "I'll take the picture back."

It wasn't what I wanted to hear. Taking the picture back meant he agreed with me. The tightness in my throat moved down to my chest.

"But I do wish you'd keep it. You are that girl, no matter what happened. It hasn't changed what you are."

I started to cry again, burying my head in his shoulder and wetting his rugby shirt. He patted me awkwardly, and kissed my hair. That only made me cry harder. "This is crazy," I mumbled against his shoulder. "I've been numb all week." I reached out for the tissue box that usually rested on the hump on the floor. It was empty. I blew into an already wet tissue. "It's crazy, wasting all this water when California's having such a drought!"

I was expecting him to laugh. Somehow I had sought the words to ease our pain. But he didn't react at all.

"It was a green Dodge Swinger, seventy-two or -three model," he mused, looking straight ahead. "There was a dent on the rear right fender. Funny I should remember that, but not the license number."

I pulled back, suddenly alert. "Do you remember how he looked? Could you identify him— maybe from pictures Corbett has?"

"I'll do better than that."

"What do you mean?"

"Nothing." David put the key in the ignition.

"What do you mean?" I repeated, getting a funny, scared feeling in the pit of my stomach.

There was something about his voice. Was he thinking of going after him, too?

David didn't answer. He started the car, released the brake, and checked the rearview mirror.

I switched off the ignition, and pulled out the key. "Tell me what you mean!" I cried. "David! Don't get any ideas. My father's already talking like a killer. You're just a kid. Leave it to the police."

"Give me the keys."

"Not till you promise."

"I'm not promising anything. You shouldn't try to make me. Now give me the keys!"

I gave him the keys, then went back to twisting the rings on my fingers.

"You have to understand, Andrea—how *I* feel. I feel so damned *guilty*, no matter what you say."

"Well, you shouldn't." I said it automatically, without much real feeling. "You know what? I'm sick of you all. Everybody. Mom, Dad, Sue, you, everybody. The only one who really cares is Jeff."

"What are you saying? I care!"

"Sure, just like they do. Nobody's really interested in how I feel, only in how *they* feel. Mom's so ashamed, she can hardly stand to look at me. Dad's angry and wants revenge. Sue understands some, but even she doesn't want to get too close to it. Since Paul dropped her, she's built a wall around her real feelings. And you! I thought you'd at least understand. But now I realize I was wrong. All that really matters to you is dealing with your guilt." I moved away from him. "It's too much, all

this worrying about the rest of you. I've got enough
trouble figuring out my own messed-up feelings.
Listen, I'm tired. Take me home now, okay?
Please?"

"It's early. Don't you want something? You
hardly ate anything." There wasn't much enthusi-
asm to his offer.

"No. It's been a long day. I just want to go
home."

David shrugged, put the key in the ignition, and
started the car. Then he pulled out into traffic. He
seemed preoccupied, and we hardly spoke all the
way back to Encino. When David took me to the
door, I opened it quickly. On early evenings like
this I'd normally ask him in. We'd go into the den
and play records and talk. Or maybe we'd concoct
some marshmallow crispies, throwing in some
peanuts and raisins and whatever other goodies
we could find in the cupboard. But tonight, I could
hardly get away fast enough. Whatever it was
David intended doing had put a barrier between
us. And so, when we reached the door, I opened it
quickly, gave David the fake smile which was
becoming a fixture on my face, and said good
night. When I looked back, just before closing the
door, David seemed bewildered. But he turned
quickly, and went down the walk, back to his car.

11

"You mean, you *told* David!" My mother's voice was shrill. She had followed me into the kitchen when I came in, leaving my father asleep in front of the TV with a rerun of *The Bob Newhart Show* playing loudly.

I was rummaging through the refrigerator, looking for something to eat. I straightened up and imitated her voice with a little extra sarcasm, and an even higher pitch. "*Yes,* I *told* David!"

"Don't you talk to *me* that way, young lady!"

"Then don't *you* talk to *me* that way!" I bent again and pulled out a jar of peanut butter, then went hunting crackers. "Aren't there any crackers, damn it! There's never anything to snack in this dumb house!"

"Whatever made you do such a stupid thing? For God's sake, why don't you take an ad out in the *Valley News*! Don't you ever listen?"

"*No,* I never listen," I went on. My voice was

close to screaming. "I always do dumb things. Like hitchhiking. Like getting raped . . ."

My mother slapped me, then clapped a hand over my mouth. "Don't you *ever* use that word in this house!"

I bit her hand and she jumped away. "Go to hell!" I threw the peanut butter jar on the counter and it broke. The pieces flew every which way. I didn't care. It didn't matter. I stomped off to my room.

She came after me. "Andrea! Open this door!" She rattled the knob angrily. "Let me in!"

"Go to hell!" Go to hell, I said again, this time to myself. I flopped down on the bed and sat facing the door, arms crossed.

"If you don't open up, I'll do it for you!" She went down the hall and into the kitchen. In a minute she was back. She must have gotten a screwdriver. The bedroom doors don't take much to unlock them. And then there she was, red-faced with fury, in front of my bed.

"This is *my* room. I have a right to privacy!" I said. "Please get out!"

She didn't move. She just stood there, with one hand, the one I'd bitten, to her mouth. The other gripped the bedpost tightly, as if for support. "I thought we'd agreed you were not going to talk about this. Before you know it, the whole neighborhood will know."

"Of all people, it seems to me David has the right to know."

"But Andrea!" She came to sit on the edge of

my bed, and turned toward me. "Don't you realize? He's liable to . . ."

I interrupted. "What? Think I'm not good enough for him anymore? Figure I'll be easier to—*lay*?"

Mother winced.

"Don't you think *I've* thought of all that already? And don't you think I want to keep it quiet more than anyone else? Do you think I want people to be looking at me and saying, 'Andrea's been—'"

"Don't say it," Mother whispered, putting a finger to my lips. "Don't say it, Andrea. Please, dear."

I shook my head. "No, I can't say it. You won't let me. That's the trouble. And I can't just plunge it out of my head, either, like you'd plunge a stopped-up toilet. I feel so awful, so dirty, so ashamed, so frightened, and even so guilty! So, what am I supposed to do? *Huh, Mom?*" I could barely control the rage inside me. And there I was, crying again, my head in my hands.

Mother smoothed my hair and let me cry. I edged closer to her and lay my head in her lap, needing the comfort of her body, wanting to crawl into her arms and be a baby again.

"There, there," she crooned. "There, there. I didn't realize." And then quietly, she added, "Maybe we ought to have some help. Maybe you ought to see someone—a psychologist or something. I just don't know how to handle this. And I guess your father doesn't either."

Corbett's words came back to me. I'd taken the card he'd given me that day and just dropped it in my purse, not intending to do anything about it. "There's a Rape Hotline in L.A." I mumbled. "Corbett gave me the number. You think I should call them?"

Mother stiffened under my head, and didn't speak for a moment. But then she finally said, "I don't know. Maybe. Perhaps you should."

Since it happened, I hadn't been sleeping well. I'd fall into an exhausted sleep but then wake suddenly, around one or two in the morning. The room would be hot because I wasn't keeping my window open at night anymore, and the only time to cool your house off in southern California is at night. But that wasn't what woke me. It was the dreams. Vague, violent dreams from which I'd wake sweaty and squirming. Almost always, I was trying to scream "help," but no sound came out.

Once awake, I'd lie in bed thinking, going over everything and wondering if maybe I should have fought back more than I did; maybe he was only trying to scare me when he said he'd kill me. I kept wondering if maybe there was something about me, the way I dressed or acted, that made him pick me. Was it possible that I really was a slut? Did men think I was looking for "it"?

So many things I'd think—like why people are so cruel to each other. How could anyone treat a human being as if he wasn't worth anything? I can't even hurt a spider. If I find one in the house, I pick it up on a piece of paper and put it outdoors.

You're supposed to love your enemy. How could I love a man who treated me like a "thing," and maybe gave me V.D., and who made me scared I might get cancer, and made me fear everything now?

Sunday morning I slept late. When I woke up there was Jeffrey sitting lotus position on the floor reading the comics. Every few seconds he looked up to see if I was awake and when he saw that I was, he smiled.

"Hi," I said, smiling back. "What time is it?"

"Late. Ten thirty."

"Where is everybody?"

"Sue's in the family room, still in pajamas, reading the paper. Mom's on the phone. She had a big argument with Daddy this morning and Daddy's gone out."

"Where to?"

"I'm not sure. He was talking about checking something, some address he got from somebody in the car agency."

"The Motor Vehicle Bureau?"

"Yeah. That's it."

I sat up. Oh, Daddy! He'd mentioned having a friend at Motor Vehicle. Could he have persuaded the man to give him the names and addresses of all green Dodges, 1972-3 models, whose owners were blond men, about thirty years old? There must be hundreds, maybe thousands. Was Daddy going to check them all out? I got out of bed and

went into the bathroom to brush my teeth. Jeffrey
followed me.

"Would you come over to the Williams's with me
later? You just have to see those pups."

Who could think of dogs now, with Daddy float-
ing around L.A. every free minute he had, checking out car owners.

"What do you think, Andrea? Sam's been dead
a long time already. You think Mom would let me
get one?"

"No."

"Why not? I could take care of it. I'm older
now."

I splashed some water on my face and tried to
talk at the same time. "She's thinking of going
back to work. She doesn't want any extra trouble
around the house."

"Everybody on the block has a dog. And the
Clarks have two. I don't see why we can't have
one."

I shrugged and dried my face.

"Will you at least come with me and look at
them?" He followed me back into the bedroom.

"Sure," I said. "Now scram. I want to get
dressed."

Jeff picked up the comics and headed for the
door, but then he stopped and looked back.
Andrea?"

"What?"

"What's—*mo*-lest mean?"

I was rummaging through my drawer for a

clean pair of shorts, and my heart began hammering. "What?"

"Mo-*lest*. One of the kids used it."

"How?"

"He said he heard his mother on the phone. She was talking about you. She said you'd been mo-*lested*."

So the news was out. It sure hadn't taken long. Now I couldn't even walk down the street without wondering if Jeff's friends were smirking about me behind my back. And if his friends knew, then their brothers and sisters did, too. At that moment I wished I could just disappear from the face of the earth.

"Andrea? What's it mean?"

"It means," I said, not looking at him, "to attack, to hurt, to assault . . ." I couldn't add the word that would give the complete meaning.

"Oh," Jeff said. "Like that man did to you."

"Yes," I said, "like that man did to me."

12

Sue was curled up on the family-room couch, reading the Sunday paper, when I came in for breakfast. "If you're making coffee, make some for me too, will you?" she asked without looking up.

I heated the water for coffee and put some English muffins in the toaster oven, then waited, staring at the heating elements as they got red and slowly browned the bread. Telling David had been such a relief. He'd been so understanding. For those few minutes I'd felt clean again, like maybe I wasn't such an ugly, defiled body. But then, he'd suddenly changed . . . that tenderness, that honest grief. It was as if releasing that grief had emptied him. What remained was like a computer, hard and reasoning, forgetting me, us, only wanting to solve its problem. I wondered even if he'd call again.

The teapot whistled. I turned it off, poured a

spoon of freeze-dried coffee into each of two cups, and put the toasted muffins on a plate. Then I stood there, staring at the coffee and muffins, forgetting what to do next. *Mo-lest.* The word shrilled in my head. I cupped my hands over my ears to stop the screaming.

"Hey, where's that coffee?"

Next thing I knew Sue's hands were on my shoulders, moving me like an automaton into the family room and a chair. She went back to the kitchen for the coffee and toast, placed them in front of me and sat down. "You better open up or you'll blow a fuse, Andrea. Come on now, talk!"

I've never really been able to confide in Sue. She's never invited it for one thing. But more important, she has this funny quirk. You tell her something and think she's understanding, being sympathetic, when *boom*! She sticks the dagger in right where it hurts.

But at that moment my defenses weren't operating. One kind word was all I needed to split wide open. I spilled out everything—David, the neighbors, the girls in the shop, Mom, everything. She listened, letting me pour it out in a monotone. Now and then she'd take a sip of coffee, her eyes fixed on my face.

"Well," she said at last, letting out a deep breath, "you *are* carrying a load." She viewed me over the coffee cup. "Okay, this is how I see it." She put down her cup, leaned her elbows on the table, and bent toward me.

"You feel guilty. You think maybe you brought

it on yourself, that maybe you were responsible for it. Bull. You made a dumb mistake is all. It really was dumb, hitching, you know. But then you never could be told anything. So maybe you learned an expensive lesson."

The soft touch, then the knife; that was Sue. Yet there was truth in what she said. I pulled at a crumb of cold muffin, kneading and rolling it into a small, round ball with two fingers.

"About those gossipy girls. Forget them. Next week they'll hear someone they know is pregnant and she'll be the topic of the day. If I worried what everyone thought about some of the things I do, well . . ." She didn't finish. "Now, about Mom. You gotta forgive her. She grew up with all these stupid hangups about virginity. She can't help the way she feels."

Before I could respond she added, "Listen. This is a world full of shit. You just swallow it and get on with living, like I did when Paul left."

"Losing a boyfriend's not quite like getting raped!"

"Oh, Andrea. Quit the Snow White bit. Don't tell me you were a virgin."

"Yes, I was!" The tears started when I met my sister's look. "I really wanted to wait . . . for someone special . . ."

Sue snorted. "Oh, wow! I can't believe it. How Victorian. Half the girls in your high school aren't virgins anymore!"

"That's not the point!" I nearly shouted. "We're not even talking about the same things! It's not love we're talking about! It's Rape. R - A - P - E! Don't you know the difference? It wasn't something I agreed to. It wasn't love! It was violence. It was hate! He threatened to kill me. I really thought he would! He wanted to hurt me, to make it as awful as possible. Sue, I was violated! Don't you understand?"

She put a hand on my arm to calm me. "Okay! Sure. It was awful for you. And he was some kind of sick pervert. Well, damn it. Stop dwelling on it. Let it go. All you've done these last four days is brood and whimper. You've got the whole family tiptoeing around like you're sick or something. You know what? I think you're just playing for sympathy!"

I jerked my arm away. "Is that what you think?" I could feel the blood drain from my head. So I'd become a burden. All I did was whimper. At that moment it seemed to me there was no place for me at home anymore.

She must have read my face because immediately she tried to take it back. "Well, no. Maybe I went too far. What I mean is, life goes on. If you stopped pitying yourself, you could deal with it. Get on with your life."

"How?"

"Do things. Don't look back. Go to a movie with Kim and don't talk about it. David's leaving for college soon, isn't he? Okay. So . . . he loves you. So?"

"So?"

She shrugged. "God. Do I have to draw you a

Gloria D. Miklowitz

diagram. If there's anyone who can erase those ugly pictures in your head, it should be him. Let him show you how nice it can really be."

"The thought of it . . . makes me want to puke."

She threw up her hands in exasperation. "Then maybe Mom's right. Maybe you do need a shrink."

I didn't answer. I just sat there nibbling my cold muffin and drinking my cold coffee and letting my head go into a deep freeze. Then nothing could hurt. Sue sat with me awhile longer, made a few futile efforts to talk about what was in the paper, finally gave up and took her cup and saucer to the dishwasher. Then she sat down on the couch again with the Sunday paper.

Sometimes you can sit quietly, not even knowing your head is working, yet it is. And that's what must have happened that day, because suddenly something inside me decided it just couldn't go on hurting like that. Maybe it's that I'm a survivor. I've always been that way. When someone closes a door on me, I don't stand there knocking my head against it till I'm bloody. I know when it's time to give up and start looking for another door to get what I need. And I guess that's what happened at that moment. I decided someplace deep inside that nobody I knew was going to help plug up my hurt. That even Mom wasn't going to hurry into finding a therapist. Her philosophy was "maybe everything will be better tomorrow." So, it had to be *me* who helped me. Okay. The first step would be to check out that Rape Hotline.

I got up and put my dishes away, got some money, then headed for the front door. Calling from home was out of the question. There were too many ears around to listen to me "whimper."

"Where you going?" Sue called as soon as I left the room.

"Out—for a walk."

Sue left the family room and came after me. "You want company?"

She really did want to help. Too bad she didn't know how. "Thanks." I flashed her my "everything's fine" smile. "I won't be long. And I'd rather go alone."

"Sure?" she asked doubtfully.

I gave her a quick hug. "Yeah, sure."

How brave to walk, to risk passing a bush behind which He might be hiding, to move steadily from Adlon to Hayvenhurst, eyeing each car suspiciously, both coming from behind and going by, alert to color, kind, whether or not it slows. I let out a breath, for now I'm on Hayvenhurst. Safe. Not on this busy street would he dare. Arms relax. Legs stop shaking. Eyes turn inward. I am safe.

The police. I wonder if they will ever find him, or if I'm just another statistic. Still, Corbett seemed sincere. A shiver rushes through me at a new thought. Supposing they do catch him. I must identify him, face him, accuse him, testify in court against him! I can't deal with that thought now, push it aside and make a resolution. No more fantasizing about running away, starting a life where no one will know me. I will not end it all, for even that cowardly solution had been played out in my head. No. I will survive, somehow.

A car. It slows. Someone leans out the window, grins, shouts. An obscenity? Oh God, why? All problems disappear and only fear remains. I start running. The car squeals as it passes; the driver honks. My heart is pounding again. I can hardly breathe, but my feet keep pumping until at last I stop, far down the road, safe, leaning against a phone pole. Bile surges into my mouth and I swallow it. I stand there heaving, panting, sick with a fear at what was probably nothing.

Calm yourself. Remember the litany against fear. I call up the words, race through them twice, three times, seeking the calm. *"Fear-is-the-mind-killer-I-must-not-fear-I-will-face-my-fear-and-where-it-has-been-there-will-be-nothing-only-me."* Calm, like the comfort of a warm bath, washes through me.

Now I find myself on Ventura Boulevard. I need help and I am going to get it! I find a drugstore open. "Got change for a dollar?" She gives me a fistful of dimes and I head for the back of the store. But the phone there offers no privacy from the people browsing among books, toothpaste, and suntan lotions. I go out again to look for a gas station. There is always a phone booth in gas stations, a place where you can close yourself into the glass box, shutting out the rest of the world.

When I pick up the receiver, I feel an urgency, like someone drowning who is offered an airhose.

"Rape Hotline, Luisa speaking. May I help you?" the voice says.

I take a deep breath, my hand sweating around the phone, and my legs like wet spaghetti. "My name is Andrea," I begin. "And I was raped."

When I don't say anything more, Luisa asks, "When, Andrea? When did it happen?" Her voice is young, like someone maybe in her twenties.

"Last week." I swallow and squinch my eyes closed. "Wednesday."

"Have you seen a doctor?"

"Yes. Right after—at the emergency hospital." I am crying now, tears salting down to my lips, and my chest is all congested.

"Would you like to talk about it? Tell me what happened. How you feel."

I do want to tell. In the hot booth, with the sweat dribbling down my neck, running between my breasts, I search for a face to the voice. In my mind's eye I see a slender woman, not too pretty, but with intelligent eyes, maybe a kind, serene face. In her few words, I feel there is someone who can listen quietly, and not interrupt except to say, "Go on. And then?" She lets me talk, lets me tell how much I hate myself for having been so stupid, hears me out as I whisper my fears and shame. Not once does she say I'm wrong or selfish or stupid. I pause, gulping the tears down, yet feeling renewed, refreshed.

"Oh, it's so good to talk like this!" I say. "My mother and sister think I'm dwelling on it too much, that I should forget it."

"No, Andrea. It's very normal. Don't suppress those feelings. You're going through a typical first-stage reaction. In a few weeks you'll think everything's okay, that you've gotten over it. Then something small can trigger the reaction all over again. If you're forced to forget what you're feeling now, it can be worse later."

I listen, feeling soothed for the first time. I even feel less angry about Sue. Luisa says it is natural for me to take her slightest harsh word as an accusation, even if she doesn't mean it to be.

We've been talking some time when Luisa asks, "What if they catch the man? Have you thought whether you'll prosecute?"

"Yes," I say. "But I don't know." I tell Luisa about my mother's reaction. "She's afraid of what people will say. She'd like to hide it, forget it ever happened, although she says it's for my sake she wouldn't want me to go to trial . . . having to expose everything before all those people."

"Umm," Luisa says. "And how do you feel?"

"I'm not sure. If they catch him, then it seems someone has to stop him. Someone has to accuse him, or he'll be out there doing it to someone else."

"That's so," Luisa agrees. "It takes a good deal of courage."

"It does." And I think about it awhile, not saying anything. I try to picture myself in a court-room, with *him* there, and maybe his wife and kids. And all those people in a jury box. And a judge, and attorneys, and spectators, and . . . *my mother and father*. I just couldn't say what I might have to say—not before the whole world, like that. Not with my mom and dad there. "I don't think I could do it," I say.

"I understand," Luisa replies. "But there's plenty of time to think about it. They have to catch him first."

My dimes are gone, and Luisa offers to call me at home. But I tell her I don't want that. That I couldn't speak freely from home.

When the operator interrupts, Luisa says she'll call me back if I give her the phone booth number. But I feel there is really no need. "You've helped a lot," I say. "I'm really grateful. I feel so much better."

"Andrea," Luisa says, before we are discon-nected. "Do you have a pencil and paper?"

"No, why?"

"I can give you names of some counseling serv-ices, or a good psychiatrist, someone who has worked with victims and knows their special problems. You need help. So do your parents."

"Yes, yes!" The operator comes on again, asking for another dime. "Just a second, operator. We're almost done," I say. But before I can say anything else, the line goes dead.

Even so, I walk away from the booth feeling good. When the gas station attendant nods my way, I wāve back. Going home, I feel like half the weights around my heart have melted away. Even though I cross the street when a man comes toward me, it's a thing accomplished with only a quick surge of adrenaline, not the heart-squeezing terror of an hour ago. I'll call again, I promised myself. Maybe I'll be all right now. Maybe the nightmare is finally over after all.

13

Two days later my mother handed me an article about a judge in Madison, Wisconsin. He tried a fifteen-year-old boy who admitted raping a girl on a stairwell of their high school. Mom was almost gleeful when I came in to breakfast. "Just look at this! That's just what I mean! Here's this poor girl attacked in her very own school, where you'd think she'd be safe, and what happens? The boy who did it is let off—scot-free! Oh sure, they'll require he stay home for a year under court supervision, and get treatment at a youth center, but what's that?"

She passed the newspaper over to me, and I read the whole story. The judge, it seemed, said the boy was just *doing what comes naturally*—that he had been overheated by newspaper ads and sex stories and all the rest. And if those things turned him on, it was "just natural" he might want to rape someone—someone like me. So what protection was there?

"Well?" my mother asked. "What do you think of that?"

"I wonder how many rapists *are* brought to trial and how many of those are convicted."

"Who cares?" Mom returned. "The fact is that you'd have to wash all that dirty laundry in court, and for what? They'd just blame it on you—say you brought it on yourself, wearing what you did!"

"I wore a shirt and jeans over my swimsuit, *Mom!* And even if I hadn't, does it give him the right to do that?"

"Promise me," my mother said, pointing a fork at me, "just promise me, Andrea, that if they catch that . . . that vile . . . creature, you won't go to trial."

I looked down at the article again and wanted to cry and scream, both at the same time.

"Andrea?" mother repeated.

"I can't," I said. "That's something I have to decide myself."

I was working at 31 Flavors the next week, feeling bad that David hadn't called and brooding over that article about the judge in Wisconsin, when Corbett came by. There I was, digging and scraping at that hard chocolate-chip ice cream thinking what a fool I'd be going to trial and letting the whole world in on what happened. The judge would say, "Sorry, kid. He couldn't help himself, what with porno magazines and X-rated films and you dressed the way you were . . ." And all of a sudden I looked up and there was Corbett watching me. He wasn't in his police uniform, so he didn't really attract attention. But when I saw him, my heart nearly dropped to my toes. Quietly, he said he'd like to see me at my break. He had some more pictures to go over with me. I glanced at Bob, but he didn't even notice. "In fifteen minutes," I said, feeling the heat rise to my face. "Out in back."

When I came out, Corbett said, "I was sorry to startle you like that, Andrea. My shift is over at four, and I did want to go over these with you." He held out a large yellow envelope. "I've pulled these photos from our mug shots because they had some similarities to your description of the man— and because these men have something of the same way of going after their victims. Take your time. I can leave them with you, if you like."

"No." I reached for the pictures. "I'll look at them now."

Corbett led me to a parked car down the alley. He pulled a folder out of the yellow envelope and laid it on a car hood. The folder had six cutout spaces, into which he had put six different men's pictures. I began to get all tense and sweaty, scared, I think, that I'd see his face.

He took a card from his wallet and read from

it. It said something about my having the right to refuse to examine the photos . . . and that if I did look at them, that I might or might not find the picture of my attacker. When I said I understood the warning, he let me see the pictures.

All the photos were front face. I studied each one carefully, knowing they might have been taken as long as five years ago or more, so if there was one of *him*, he wouldn't look quite the same. But his face was engraved in my memory, despite the thousands of pictures Corbett had already shown me, and none of those he brought were him.

"What if this was his first time?"

"That makes it a bit harder," Corbett admitted.

As we walked back to the store, he said he'd keep trying. And then I asked him, "How often do you catch one of these guys?"

"Well." He scratched his head. "I saw some statistics on that recently. Don't hold me to them —but it seems to me there were something like fifty-six thousand reported rapes in the United States last year, and about twenty-five percent of those resulted in arrests. That's only the tip of the iceberg, though. I'd guess that only one in ten rapes are ever reported."

"Yeah. I can see why. Why bother, if the guy gets off like the one in the newspaper this morning."

"I saw that," Corbett said. "The judge should be

thrown off the bench. Don't go by that verdict, though, or you'll never want to go to trial."

"I don't intend to." Until that minute, I hadn't realized I'd made a decision.

"I hope you don't mean that."

"I do."

"You mean, when we catch him . . ."

"You mean *if* you catch him."

"All right, *if*. . . . You mean you'd waste all our efforts? You know, we can't put him where he belongs without your help, or the help of other victims."

I was at the back door, with my hand on the knob, and turned to Corbett, putting all the anger I felt into my words. "Would *you*? Under the circumstances? Would you advise *your* daughter to go through a trial when he'll probably be let off with an apology from the judge that *he couldn't help it*. He was just doing *'what comes naturally'*!"

"Andrea," Corbett said. "You don't prosecute, and you carry that anger around inside you like a time bomb . . . because there's just no other way to get back at that guy."

"Okay . . . so say I accuse him and go through with a trial. . . . What are the statistics then, Officer Corbett?" I drew the words out with all the sarcasm I could muster. "Of those—what—a fourth of fifty-six thousand is fourteen thousand. Fourteen thousand arrests. Just how many went to jail?"

Corbett cleared his throat and looked embarrassed. "The rate of conviction is getting better every year."

"You didn't answer my question!"

"Well, not many."

"*How* many?"

He cleared his throat again and looked away. "Uh—about one in sixty are convicted."

"One in sixty?" My voice went shrill.

"That's not the whole story. Maybe another one in forty get probation and some county-jail time."

I could hear a strangled sound come from my throat. There was nothing more to say. I opened the back door to the store and went in. Behind me I heard Corbett add, "But Andrea, the conviction rate gets better every year!"

By the next week things were beginning to settle into place. I began calling Luisa whenever the pressures built up too much in my head. She suggested I try writing it all down, but I was too close to it then.

Although I was still mixed up and angry, unburdening myself on the phone helped. So did work, which took part of each day. And happily, my period started. I don't know when I've been more relieved. Though there was still one more V.D. test to take, I'd begun to believe it would turn out negative. So as long as I could keep myself from brooding, there were times when I almost believed it had never happened.

At home, on the surface at least, things looked

normal. Sue and I returned to our usual relationship. Mom went around with this cheerful smile around her lips while her eyes looked wary and sad. She seemed especially interested in what I wore when I left the house. But as long as I didn't stay in my room too much, she was ready to believe everything was back to normal.

David hadn't called yet. That hurt. All right, I thought, if that's how you feel—fine. But of course it wasn't fine. It hurt terribly.

Daddy wasn't the same, either. The first week he was out nearly every night till late, checking off that list he carried with him all the time. Mom never said anything, but she was always asking the time until he got home. I don't think she could have stopped him anyway. She'd said everything she could to dissuade him. I heard their loud arguments, even though their bedroom door was closed.

By the second week Dad was letting up. He was coming home from work after dark, using the daylight hours to check, I suppose, but he stayed home after that. He seemed apologetic, not quite able to be comfortable with me, as if he thought I expected him to be out there playing detective.

I'd refused a call from Kim the day after the attack, because I couldn't bear to talk to her. But then she didn't call again. I didn't like to think why. Once we'd been good friends, though we hadn't seen much of each other since I started seeing David. I figured she'd thought it over and

just couldn't be comfortable around me anymore.

But the second week, she called twice. Now, I
figured, Karen and Cindy must have gotten to her,
asking her to do their dirty work and get the
nitty-gritty details from me.

"Tell her I'm not in, Mom. She's only curious."

"How do you know? Are you going to be suspicious of everyone who calls?"

"Look, take my word for it. She's only prying."

The second time, though, one look from my
mother and I decided I'd better get it over with.
Mom was nearby, doing needlepoint, and I knew
she'd be listening. Well, here goes, I thought,
picking up the phone like it was a live rattlesnake.

"Hi, Andrea! It's me, Kim."

"Hi," I said without warmth.

"How are you?"

"Fine."

"I'm glad." She was quiet a moment and I could
picture her face, pale and serious, with the deep
blue eyes of her father. Her kindness the day of
the rape had been genuine, but in my untrusting
state, my guard was up.

"I just wanted you to know," she went on, "that
I wasn't in on that visit when Karen and Cindy
came to see you. They asked me to go along, but
I wouldn't."

"Too bad. Think of the fun you missed." Bull, I
thought. So how come it took you over a week to
tell me so!

"Look. I would have called before this, but we've been away. We were camping in Baja all last week." When I didn't say anything, she added, "How do you like your job? You still into Mocha Almond Fudge?"

I began to think maybe I was being too mean, so I decided to help the conversation along. "It's fine, and no on the ice cream. What are you doing for the rest of the summer?"

"Teaching little kids to swim. I've got a fourteen-month-old baby in one class. Can you imagine?"

"That's fantastic." The words seemed to be coming from some remote part of me.

"Well, I just called to find out how you were." She paused. "Would you like to come over to swim some time? We have an olympic-size pool."

"I know. Maybe sometime."

"I'm only two blocks away. How about tomorrow?"

Don't push me, I thought. "I think I'm busy. I'll let you know."

"That was thoughtful of Kim to call," my mother said, afterward. "What did she want?"

"She invited me to go swimming tomorrow."

"Isn't that nice. You'll go, of course."

"I don't think so."

Mother's lips got that tight, sour look she gets when she's angry. She bent over her needlepoint. "How come David hasn't been around?" she asked.

"I guess he's busy."

"Has he called?"

"No! What is this—the third degree? If I want to go swimming, that's my business. And what's this sudden interest in David, anyway? You couldn't have cared less if he called—*before!*"

"I was just wondering." Mom glanced up. Her eyes looked tired. "My, you are touchy!"

"That's right! I sure am! Do you wonder?" I dropped into a chair and grabbed a magazine. "I'm plain sick of your checking on me so much!"

Mom didn't answer. She just returned to her needlepoint while I buried my face behind the magazine, thinking about David. I'd been mean, talking to Mom that way, but her question had touched a nerve. David would be leaving for college soon. I marked the days off in my head, conscious that time was running out. Before, we'd expected to spend every spare hour together till he left.

His not calling took on more importance each day. It seemed obvious that he'd had time to think about what happened to me and just couldn't stomach a girl friend who was *used*. Used was the kindest word I tossed around in my head. There were a lot of juicier ones, words the kids at school would have loved chewing over, and school was starting in another week or two.

But there was more to it than fearing what he thought of me. Though I wanted David to call and reassure me, I didn't want *to see him*, not the way it had been. It had to do with fear of being touched. I couldn't return to the way it was.

Kissing, touching, all that stuff that used to make me all warm and soft inside seemed revolting now. I guess it was better he didn't call.

Well, one thing for sure, I decided. I wouldn't call him.

14

It was because of Mrs. Hoffman that I broke my
promise and called David.

I'd only met Mrs. Hoffman once, when she gave
a surprise party for David's eighteenth birthday.
She'd been friendly enough, but treated me just
like any other of David's friends, so when I heard
she'd called, I was naturally curious to know why.

"It's about David," Mrs. Hoffman said when I
returned her call. "Have you been seeing much of
him lately?"

"Not lately." I was puzzled by the question. "In
fact not for a week and a half. Why?"

"Oh," Mrs. Hoffman returned, almost as if she
was disappointed. "I thought maybe he was spending more time with you." She paused. "Then I
don't know what to think."

"What do you mean?"

"Well, I don't really want to burden you with this, but David's been acting strange. I don't think he's been working at his job, for one thing—at least not in the afternoons."

"What makes you think that?"

Mrs. Hoffman didn't answer immediately. Then she said, "The Fuller area manager called. He said David hadn't picked up the orders he was supposed to deliver. I reminded David twice, but it was like talking to a wall. He just seemed so far away. It's not like him to neglect his responsibilities."

"He's probably just busy selling," I offered.

"I don't think so. When he comes home evenings, we ask him how he did. If we don't ask, he usually tells us . . . because he's been trying to outdo his record each week. He's trying to help with his college expenses, you know. Well, this last week, when we ask, he says—'Okay' . . . then he rushes off to his room."

I remembered with a spurt of fear David's sudden secretive attitude in the car.

"Perhaps it's nothing, but he's not selling Fuller Brushes in the hours he's away from home. At least I don't think so."

I didn't answer.

"We never pry . . . but I've been so worried about David's change in behavior that my husband checked his room. He saw his order form for the last two weeks. He hardly sold anything."

Oh, *damn*, David . . . what are you up to? I

thought. Why haven't you called, and what are you doing with your days, if not working? "Did you *ask* him?"

Mrs. Hoffman's voice dropped. "No, because I don't want him to know we've been spying. And because we'd like to believe, if he *was* in any trouble, he would come to us." Then Mrs. Hoffman said, "Andrea? Would you call him? Speak to him? I'd be most grateful. He thinks so highly of you. Maybe he'll tell you."

It's funny—sometimes if you're really troubled, it's good to be distracted by someone else's problems. For a while, at least, you forget yourself. Thinking about David and what trouble he might be in, what I could say, how he'd respond, took me out of myself.

When I called, he seemed in a hurry, said he'd drive me to work the next day, and we could talk then. I was on the afternoon shift, 3–8 P.M., the time David was usually out door-to-dooring. "Why do that?" I said, thinking how his route was in the opposite direction. "Then you'll have to drive all the way back again."

"That's my worry. *You* sound just like your mother now."

His tone was impatient, almost rude, so I gave it right back to him. "Well, don't bother."

"Oh, *Andrea*," he said wearily. "Let's not play games."

I hesitated, not sure exactly what he meant, but then I finally said sharply, "Well, okay."

*   *   *

I settled into the front seat of his car, not close to him as I normally would, but close to the window, keeping my hands tightly folded in my lap. How can you feel so close to someone one day, and then a week later—it's as if you hardly know the person? Is it the weather, or hormones, or what happens to each of you in between? Are relationships that fragile?

We drove for a while without saying a word. My head was buzzing with ways to start the conversation, but David seemed far away and it was as awkward as a first date.

Finally I blurted the one thing I swore not to ask. *"Why haven't you called?"* It sounded accusing, almost tearful, and I would have given anything to take it back.

"Because I couldn't. Not till I made it up to you," he said, eyes straight ahead.

"What? David, there's nothing to make up!"

The muscles in his neck tightened, and he gave me a quick, pained look.

"David, what are you doing? What's going on?"

"I'm trying to get his license number. I'm trying to find him. That's all."

"But *how?"*

His Adam's apple moved up and down. "I'm looking."

"For what?"

"Simple. I just stand at that street corner where he picked us up and scan the cars passing. I figure if he came that way once, he may come through there regularly."

"That's crazy."

"No it's not. I think I'd recognize that car as soon as it came near. And I'd sure recognize him. And when I do, I'll get that license number. That's all there is to it."

"So that's how you're spending your time! So *that's* why you drove me here! You're going on to Santa Monica now!"

"Right."

"Oh, *David!*" I cried, hopelessly.

I was touched, I guess, by his intensity, and by his honest, good intentions. But shocked, too, at the way what had happened to me had affected him. Sweet, fun-loving David, standing each day for hours on a street corner—watching cars go by! It was crazy, incredible, mad!

I turned to face him, aware that he had not looked my way once since we'd started the drive. "You can just stop playing Columbo," I said, hearing a quaver in my voice. "My dad's already into that act. The police don't need any more experts."

"Sure," David said. "I should listen to you, like I listened that day."

"Well, you better listen now. Because I'm telling you, David. Even if you spot the car, it won't do any good. Because . . . I'm *not* going to press charges!"

His head flew around, and his eyes went wide. "What?" The car swerved, but he brought it back quickly.

"You heard me right."

"I don't believe it. I thought you had guts! You wouldn't be so chicken!"

I told him about the article in the newspaper and the talk with Corbett.

"I don't care about the judge. He's not typical. And as for Corbett—he's quoting old statistics."

"Last year is *old*? And the judge in Madison, Wisconsin, was *this* year . . . this month!"

By now we had pulled off the freeway and were turning up Westwood Boulevard. David had to watch the traffic because it's fierce the way cars jockey for position along there, so he didn't answer immediately.

He pulled into the alley beside 31 Flavors, jerked on the brake, and killed the motor. Then he turned to face me fully. "Andrea," he said with careful, deliberate patience, "if they catch that guy, you can't just let him go. He might go out again and hurt somebody else. You just can't."

"Oh yes I can. Besides, they'll never catch him!" The realization that I really believed this hit me, and I wanted to cry.

"But they could."

The tears started down my cheek. "You wouldn't want me to go into a courtroom and tell all those strangers what he did to me. David, you couldn't hate me that much!"

David wiped my tears away with a finger. "You know I don't hate you."

"You do! *You didn't call!* Everything's changed between us! You're ashamed of how you feel, but you do feel different! Admit it!"

"I don't. I don't, Andrea. Really. It's just that I've been so wrapped up in wanting to find that guy." He reached out to pull me close, but I didn't respond. "Andrea," he said softly. "Nothing's changed. I still love you."

I pulled at a thread on my jeans, not looking at him. "Then stop this crazy thing you're doing. It scares me. It's just not the *you* I know and like."

He put his hand on mine. "If I stop . . . will you promise something, too?"

"What?" I looked up to see his serious, dark eyes watching me.

"If they catch the guy . . . you *will* take it to trial. I'll testify, too, if it will help."

"I don't know."

"You've got to promise, or I don't promise either."

"Maybe."

"Look," David said. "I leave for school in a little over a week. And you start school soon after. Time's running out. If I'm to help, it has to be now—because I won't be around later. Andrea. Let me help you put it behind you. Let's take up where we left off."

I got this sick, lost feeling in the pit of my stomach at the thought of his leaving. "All right, I'll try." I said.

David smiled a relieved, big grin, and I smiled back. "We'll start all over again. Tomorrow—we'll go to that art exhibit at UCLA I've been wanting to see. Then . . . the Venice Noodle Factory for dinner. Then . . ." His voice deepened, and he quickly kissed my cheek. "Then, who knows . . ."

A cold sweat broke out all over me, and I ran a hand over my chilled arm. "Sure." I opened the car door and practically flew out of the car. Then, ashamed, I came round to the driver's side, to try to make amends. "Time to get back to the ice-cream works," I said, keeping my voice light. "Bye. Tomorrow, okay?"

David watched me until I got to the back door of 31 Flavors and opened it. Then we blew each other kisses, and I went in.

I dressed for my date with David as carefully as if I was going to a formal. All of a sudden, each article of clothing took on a sexual meaning. Should I wear the sundress, with the thin straps and smocked top? Or would that be an invitation to undressing me? Should I wear the white jeans and blue tank top? Did it make my breasts too obvious? See what I mean? There was of course the possibility that I bought clothes that did emphasize any sexiness. But if I did, I hadn't been aware of it. Now I looked at each article of clothing critically, with just that question in mind.

But beyond the fears about dressing, there were other thoughts jumping around in my head. What if David began to make love to me like he had before? Did I want it? Could I bear to have him touch me? Did he think perhaps that it didn't really matter now, if we did or didn't? I stood in front of the mirror, my arms wrapped around myself, frowning at the image, forcing back flickers of *him*, his huge tongue in my mouth, his hands pulling, tearing, his organ—forcing . . . and began to retch.

"Andrea Cranston," I said to my image sometime later. "Pull yourself together. You're going out with David tonight, and you're going to have a wonderful time. You're going to laugh, and talk about everything except—*that*. And then, when he kisses you, you're going to close your eyes *and enjoy it*. You've got to. You've got to blot out everything else. Because if you don't—it'll be even harder the next time. And if you can't . . . if you let *him* come between you, you're lost, really lost. You'll be linked to that man—*forever*."

It was a modern-art exhibit. I don't know a thing about what makes a good painting. In fact sometimes I think some artists are just pulling a big joke on the public. I mean, how can a big square of off-white on a white background be art?

Even so, it was fun looking at all those weird, modern paintings and sandpiles, and cord art, because it made you see there was beauty in things around you that are so commonplace you rarely think of them as art.

We browsed leisurely through the museum, stopping to giggle at something or trying to figure out what it was. And it was comfortable. I didn't even mind when David put an arm around my waist, because my mind was on other things.

"Did you ever think you'd want to be an artist,

David?" I asked. "You have the long fingers and hands of an artist . . . or at least someone creative. I read a book on palmistry once."

"I nearly flunked kindergarten," David said seriously. "Got a D minus in fingerpainting."

I laughed. "I have an idea. Let's get back at the system . . . and leave our mark here!"

"How? What do you mean?" David looked at me quizzically, but then he got the idea and a slow grin spread over his tanned face. He grabbed my hand and pulled me along. "I know just the place!"

We ran through the galleries, always slowing to a decorous pace when we saw a guard ahead, keeping straight faces until we passed. Then we rushed on again. I didn't know where we were going, but it was obvious David did.

Finally we arrived at a room we had passed earlier. It wasn't quite a room, more a "space," and there was no art hung in it at all. The three walls were bare, the carpet was bare, and the only thing there was a tall-backed chair at the far end of the room.

We stood there, hand in hand, like conspirators, looking into the room. "Are you thinking what I'm thinking?" David asked, his eyes sparkling.

I put a finger to my lip and pretended to study the space. "Well," I drew out . . . "perhaps. It has possibilities."

A guard passed by, giving us a suspicious look, and I smiled at him innocently.

"It's perfect!" David whispered.

"Let's give it a name. Here!" I rummaged in my purse and found a pencil and small pad.

"We'll need Scotch tape . . ." David said, immediately seeing my purpose. "Or a rubber band. Or some string . . ."

I rummaged some more, after passing the pad and pencil to David, and came up with an old, stretched-out rubber band. "Here. Will this do?"

David nodded. The guard passed again, and we both smiled at him, and then, reading each other's minds, walked slowly in the other direction. But as soon as he moved on, we hurried back. "What shall we call it?" David asked.

I thought. *"Chair?"* No. *"Riddle for Posterity?"*

David wet the end of the pencil to his tongue. "I've got it!" He went to the wall so he could lean the pad against it, and began writing.

I peered around, and under his arm to see what he had done. He was lettering "WISDOM AND INNOCENCE—A STUDY" in neat, large print across the top of the three-by-five sheet.

I giggled. "Now add: 'Andrea and David. 1979'!"

He added the words, tore the sheet off the pad, and held it up for me to see. "Okay, Picasso. Where's the stickum?"

I ceremoniously handed him the rubber band. Then, together, we solemnly approached the lone chair. With great care, David fixed the small paper to the top front of the chair, holding it in place with the stretched-out band.

"Oh, it's so neat!" I crowed, almost dancing with delight. "We're going to be immortal!"

"Perspective," David announced. "Most art doesn't look good close up. Stand back and observe!"

With the utmost seriousness, we stepped back to the entrance and looked. There, for all the world to see and admire, was our contribution to the museum. *Wisdom and Innocence: A Study.* By Andrea and David. 1979. I squeezed David's hand, and he kissed my head. Then, we scrambled off like two fugitives from justice, hearts pounding, not stopping till we reached the outside.

Breathless, and bubbling with laughter, we hugged each other. "You know what?" David said as we started away, "our chair is the best thing in there."

From the museum we drove to Venice to the Old Noodle Factory. It's an Italian restaurant decorated in early 1900s style. The food is good, but you could love the place just for its atmosphere. In the parlor waiting-room you find wooden signs offering beer at five cents a mug, and posters of old movies. There's a barber's chair there, and a nickelodeon, and the afternoon light filters through high, stained-glass windows. And the food—yum—especially the warm, crusty loaves of French bread served with the salad. I could fill up just on that.

David talked about Brandeis, the college he was going to in Massachusetts. The catalog had arrived that week, and he could hardly wait to sign up for the courses he wanted the first term: music, French, math, English, and a psych class. He'd be working, too, ten hours a week, to help pay his own way.

"You'll be too busy to think of me," I said, running a finger along the beads of water on the outside of my water glass. I looked up. "You won't be back till Christmas. That's four whole months. You'll find somebody else . . ."

"I'll be so busy with school and working, there won't be time for anyone else. Besides, you're my girl, aren't you?"

"Am I? Even after . . . what happened?" The words were out before I could stop them. They must have been lurking there, waiting to be asked, because it wasn't at all what I was thinking.

"*Still*—not *even* after." David lowered his voice, and took my hand across the table. "Andrea, listen. I've been reading about victims . . . about how they react."

"I don't want to talk about it. I promised myself we wouldn't get on that subject at all tonight. Please, don't!"

"I think you *should* talk about it. I think you should listen to what I learned."

I covered my ears with my hands and shook my head. "You'll spoil the whole evening. Don't."

"All right," David said. "We won't. What *do* you want to talk about?"

"Anything but that. Here. Give me your palm. I'll read your fortune."

David reached a cautious hand out, palm up, and moved closer to me. I took his hand in mine, and pretended to study it carefully. I'd read this book on palmistry, but really, without the words before me, I couldn't remember a whole lot about what the different lines meant. Still, knowing what I did about David, I started improvising.

"See . . . the way your thumb curves out? That means you're very generous."

"Definitely," David agreed.

"And here, it says you'll live to . . . one hundred and three. But at ninety-eight you'll have a serious illness . . . the flu. . . ."

"What about my love life?" David asked. "What's it say about that?"

"Not so fast. Here," I drew my finger over a line. "It shows that you will be very successful in two careers." I paused. "But my goodness! Look at *this*!"

"What?" David asked anxiously.

"Oh, David! I can't believe it."

"What?!"

"*Five* wives. Five!"

"What? Where does it show that?" When he realized I was joking, he put his left hand over mine and squeezed hard. "Oh, you! For a while you really had me believing."

Finally we left the restaurant. I'd put off leaving as long as possible, conscious of a growing anxiety at what I knew would come next. It was a little like someone about to do something very dangerous. Ahead was a deep chasm. I knew it was there. I didn't know if I could leap over it. If I jumped that chasm, I'd be okay. If I hesitated even the slightest, I'd fall into that deep abyss.

David took my hand, and we headed toward the beach a block away. I can't remember what we talked about, only that my mind was searching ahead for subjects to discuss, anything that would keep things from getting quiet, keep David from getting close.

For a while we walked along the bikepath that runs along the beach. It's well lighted, with benches along the way. David suggested going out onto the beach, but I said I'd rather not. I'd never been afraid before, but I was afraid now. Of David. Of *men* who might be there.

After a time we sat and looked out across the sand. Moonlight gave the beach a shadowy look. Ahead, to where we could barely see, the surf surged and pounded, and that wonderful sea-weedy, fishy, salty smell came to us. I shivered.

"Cold?" David put an arm around my shoulder and drew me closer.

"No," I said, not withdrawing, but not relaxing either.

He took his jacket off and put it around my shoulders. "Come on. We'll walk. It's warmer that way."

He started onto the beach, and I followed, not wanting to, but unable to say no. When we took off our shoes, David ran back to put them under the bench. Watching him, I was conscious that the clock to the bomb had been set now; there was no stopping it.

Near the shore, sandpipers picked their way over the wet beach, leaving tracks that disappeared as quickly as they were set down. Gulls, dark and shadowy over the ocean, dove seaward like dropping weights; over the roar of the surf you could hear their shrieks.

The wet sand was cold, and I could feel the sea-spray on my face and hair. David put his arms around me. With my face against his chest, I smelled the faint scent of after-shave lotion, and felt his heart beating against my cheek. "Better?" he asked.

I nodded, but kept my face averted.

"Cold . . . or *afraid?*"

I looked up then, feeling the tears begin in my eyes. And he kissed me. First on the forehead, then on the nose, and then on the lips. Cool, brotherly kisses, at first, but then increasingly serious and intense. And I kept myself apart, knowing precisely what he was doing, and not wanting to become a part of it, not daring to feel anything. To feel was to risk remembering the revulsion, the hate and fear.

Presently he drew me up to the dry sand. There he laid out his jacket and, taking my hand, pulled me down beside him. I trembled, wanting to run. But he didn't touch me. He sat with his hands hugging his knees, and stared out at the water.

"There are three ways of dealing with what happened to you," David said quietly. "I've been reading about it. And you've got to listen." He rushed on before I could stop him. "There's denying it ever happened, which I imagine you try to do . . . considering no one at home wants to acknowledge it. There's becoming promiscuous . . . because you feel worthless. Or . . ." He glanced quickly my way. "The opposite. There's becoming frigid. . . ."

I must not fear, I thought to myself, closing my eyes. *Fear is the mind-killer.* . . . I hugged my arms around myself and heard my teeth chattering, but not from cold.

"Andrea. Let me help you. Let me try. I'll stop anytime you say." Gently, he laid me down so my head was on his jacket, and began to kiss me.

At first I withdrew, keeping my mouth hard and closed, repeating my litany in frantic silence. But he persisted, softly, slowly, as if we had forever, bringing me along, breaking through the ice of fear, gentling, until it was as sweet and wonderful as it had ever been before. Thought ceased, and the memory of *him* faded, and there was only David and me, caring, enjoying, loving each other.

It was David who stopped. He sat up suddenly, breaking away from me as abruptly as a slap. He was breathing hard and didn't speak. "David . . . don't stop . . ." I said in a very small voice.

He shook his head.

I sat up and leaned against his shoulder. "What is it?"

"I think we should go."

"Why?"

He picked up a handful of sand and dripped it on his leg. "Nothing's changed. There's no reason for you to go all the way now, just because of what happened. The reasons you had before . . . about not going too far . . . should be just as important now."

I didn't answer him. I felt ashamed that I had been willing, and it was he who had set me straight.

"I love you, Andrea," David said, not looking at me. "I wouldn't do anything in the world to hurt you."

"I know that."

"But I'm going away soon. And I won't be around when you need me. And I don't know how you'll feel about me in four months. We're young. A lot of things can happen."

"I love you, too. In four months I won't feel any different."

He kissed me lightly on the forehead. "I hope not. But in the meantime I think we shouldn't hurry things. You need time to sort out what's happened. Let's wait." He got up and helped me to my feet.

I loved him then more than anyone I had ever known. I think, if he hadn't stopped, there would have been in my mind always the thought that he figured it no longer mattered. This way, he was treating me as if . . . I was still a virgin. And I think—in *his* heart, I was.

16

The week before David went off to college seemed to fly by. I almost began to believe everything would be all right. Going to work on the bus wasn't the ordeal it was at first. I was still cautious about who I sat next to and I certainly didn't speak with strangers anymore, but the terror was gone. I still had nightmares, but not every night. And knowing I'd be seeing David after work made the days pass quickly.

At home my happier mood made everyone relax. It was almost as if it had never happened. I didn't call the Rape Hotline again, and Mom gave up on the notion that I needed to see a therapist. Sue and I began to get along—maybe because the spotlight was off me, and maybe because I was less edgy. Even Jeffrey was happier. I had convinced Mom and Dad to take him to a dermatologist and have the warts removed. He'd already seen the doctor twice, and though his hands had lots of little black-and-brown scabs, a few had already come off and the skin underneath was pink and smooth.

The day David left, I went with him and his parents to International Airport. It was a night flight and there was a big crowd waiting to board the huge 747. We were all standing together, trying to find last-minute things to say. David's mother was looking weepy, and every few seconds she'd ask if he remembered to take his blue sweater, or his tennis racket, or the new bathrobe she'd bought him. His dad finally said, "Phyllis, stop hassling him. He's not a baby anymore. He'll manage just fine without us." He put a hand on David's arm, and squeezed it affectionately.

When the boarding announcement came, everyone started to line up. David looked at me, and then said to his parents, "Listen. It's still fifteen minutes to takeoff. Andrea and I will be back in a few minutes." He grabbed my arm and we hurried away.

"Don't lose track of the time, David!" his mother called after him.

There's really no place at the American Airlines terminal that's private, so we had to settle for a wall near the escalators, where the traffic wasn't quite so heavy. I leaned against the wall, and David put a protective arm against it, making a circle of us.

"My stomach's twitching like it has Mexican jumping beans in it," he said. "I'm scared about going, and dying to go, and not wanting to leave you, and wishing I was there already!"

I was conscious of every second ticking by, and feeling just as he described. "Oh, David, how will I stand it? What will I do without you?"

With one finger he traced my lips and pushed a strand of my hair back. "Time will pass, and it will be Christmas before you know it. And I'll write—often. . . ."

A loudspeaker announced that passengers for American Airlines Flight 11 were requested to go to the boarding gate. David looked up, listening, and then looked at his watch. "We still have eight minutes."

My throat had that tight, about-to-cry feeling, and I put my arms around his waist, wishing I could hold him there forever.

We kissed a long, sweet kiss, and it didn't even matter that there were people nearby who could see. Then I said, "Come on. We better go." Hand in hand, we returned to his parents at the boarding gate, said good-bye one more time, and then he was gone.

I thought everything was going to be all right. But the week before school, soon after David left, we went to Newport. And that's when I realized how superficial the healing was, how sometimes things get worse before they can get better.

Daddy had rented the same house we'd had the year before at Newport Beach. We all looked forward to going. Normally I love the place. We sleep

late, sun on the beach, play tennis, and ride bikes.
In the afternoons we'd go into Balboa across the
bay where Sue and I would fool around with other
kids: some new friends, some from other sum-
mers. We'd have ice cream, maybe, and arrange
to get together in the evening for a beach party or
just some talk.

But this year things were different for me. Newport is full of kids my age. Lots of the older guys
pool their summer earnings and rent beach places
for a week or two, without parents, so the streets
are crawling with guys on the make and girls
looking for a good time. You don't even have to be
especially gorgeous to get attention. Just a bikini
and a suntan qualifies anyone.

The year before, when I was fourteen, I'd
looked around and wished I was older. I thought,
wow—this place is where it all happens. But this
year, Newport made me uneasy. Maybe it was the
openness, the freedom, the lack of predictability.
One morning I was on the way to the beach, when
a Porsche pulled up alongside me. The driver
whistled and said, "Hey, foxy . . . want a ride?" I
immediately got a tight, cold feeling inside, and
was hardly able to swallow. I started walking fast.
But the guy didn't take the hint. He kept cruising,
following along, offering to take me wherever I
was going. "Leave me alone!" I screamed. Then I
took off like a rabbit and ran nonstop right back
to the beachhouse.

"What's wrong?" Mom asked, when I fell into

her arms. She shook me, trying to get me to talk sense. "What happened?"

When I told her, she said, "For God's sake! Is that all? So someone whistled at you! It won't be the last time!"

"But I thought . . . I thought . . ." I said.

"You thought what?" she answered sharply. "I thought you weren't *going* to think that anymore! You can't go around suspecting every male who looks at you. That's stupid!"

Stupid or not, I was scared. Standing in front of a boutique the first afternoon, I felt someone tap me on the shoulder. My heart began pumping like I'd just run the marathon, and my legs went weak. I swung around ready to jam my fist into the someone's groin. The look on my face must have given me away, because the guy standing there backed off like he'd touched fire. His grin disappeared and he said, "Well . . . sor-*ry*! I just wanted to know if you had the time!"

"Just keep your hands to yourself, mister!" I said, hearing the hysteria in my voice. "You just keep your hands to yourself!"

"Well, sorry!" he repeated, putting his hands up in front of his face. "Man—you'd think I was trying to rape you!"

After that episode I stopped going out alone. For one thing, I began to imagine that every green car parked along the curb, or passing by, maybe was *his*. For another, I figured that telling anyone at home about these fears wouldn't do much good.

They'd just say it was silly. So I took the easy way out. I'd just wait till my parents went to the beach and tag along. "For goodness' sake," Mother said. "Even Jeffrey goes to the beach alone. What's this sudden togetherness?"

"You don't want me along? Okay. I'll stay at the house," I answered. Mom gave Dad a funny look, and then said, "Oh, don't be silly. Of course come along!"

At the beach I'd stay pretty close to the family circle. Sue had found a crowd of friends, and the one time I'd hung around, I nearly threw up when this touchy-feely type came up behind me and put his arms around my waist. I dug my fingernails into his hands and pried him loose so fast, he fell down in the sand. "Hey, what's with *you*?" he asked. I didn't answer. I just ran back to where my parents were and sat under their beach umbrella pretending to read for the rest of the day.

Sitting there, eyes fixed on the page, I tried to sort out why I was still running so scared. I thought I'd gotten over it, with David's help. Flirting used to be fun; now it terrified me. Newport seemed an arena with packs of predatory animals sniffing at the bait—me. David had insulated me from other men, but he was gone now. And I was on my own.

Even school was no longer the same. The very first day I was in the washroom with Kim. We were combing our hair. This girl came out of a stall, stopped right in front of me and said, "Say, aren't you the girl who was raped?" And here we were in this room full of other kids. It got so silent, you'd think we were in church. "What makes you think that?" I managed to mumble, feeling my face start to burn.

"Oh, well," she said. "A friend of mine is a friend of a friend of yours and she said it happened during the summer and <u>that</u> she picked you up right after. Was it you?"

"No."

"Would you tell me if it was?"

"No. It's none of your business. Why do you want to know anyway?"

"Oh, I bet it was you!" she said.

Kim took off a shoe and made like she was going to throw it at her. The girl ducked then ran for the door. Kim threw the shoe anyway.

I started keeping pretty much to myself after that. I no longer quite trusted girls, except for Kim. Oh, I'd be with other girls at lunch, but I didn't join in as I used to. I felt they might pry.

As for the guys, I didn't know what to think. One day after school while I was waiting for the bus, a boy I'd hardly ever spoken to—Eric—came up to me. He was real friendly. "Hey, Andrea," he said. "How's it going?" Then he put his hand on my arm like we'd been going together forever.

I backed off, moving so fast that I nearly knocked a girl down. Then, trying to cover my fear, I clutched my books to my chest and smiled up at him. David and I had agreed to date other people, but so far I'd never given anyone a chance to ask.

"Hey, you busy Saturday night?" Eric asked. "There's a movie I've been wanting to see."

"Which one?" I was vaguely conscious that some of his friends were standing nearby, watching us.

He mentioned an X-rated film I'd heard about, and immediately I realized what he was up to. I wondered if any of the kids around me were listening. He went on and on about what a terrific film it was and how he could borrow his sister's I.D. to get me in. The words swirled around me and I just stood there, watching his lips move and wishing I could die. All of a sudden I said, "Excuse me!" and shoved by him, pushing and running through the hordes of kids going home until I reached the bathroom. I just sat on a toilet-seat lid with the door locked and concentrated on not vomiting. It seemed to me the other guys had surely put him up to it. I could imagine what they thought he could do with me . . . if I'd accepted.

Between being careful with the girls and staying away from the guys, I'd gotten a reputation for being stuck-up. Me, the friendly-puppy type . . . stuck-up. That was a laugh. But Kim knew. I stuck to myself because I didn't want pity. And I didn't want to be talked about . . . or touched. All I wanted was to be like I had been before . . .

17

I guess the straw that broke the camel's back, to
use a cliché, was what happened one Saturday.
It was a couple of weeks after school started. Mom
had put off seeing about a therapist and it really
seemed I didn't need one. I mean, I no longer
slept ten to twelve hours a night to escape. The
nightmares came less often. Sure, I was a bit aloof
at school, but I'd stopped thinking that every
cluster of kids automatically had to be talking
about me. Kim and I even went to a party, and I
survived. It really did seem like I was getting
better.

But then that Saturday, just before Thanks-
giving, everything fell apart. One moment I was
almost as good as new—the next I felt split wide
open again.

Kim and I had planned some Christmas shopping. She was looking for a pink angora sweater,

and I planned on checking out an art shop I liked.
I hoped to find an Escher print as a Christmas
present for David. At the last minute Sue joined
us. After shopping, we figured we'd have lunch,
then go to one of the Westwood movies.

Sue drove, and rather than fight to find a parking spot in the Village, we left the car in the
Bullocks garage and started walking to the falafel
place a couple of blocks away. We were yakking
about our purchases—Sue got this terrific halter
dress and Kim found her sweater—when my eye
caught a green car passing . . . *with a dent in its
rear right fender*. I think it was the dent that
caught my eye first.

It's him, I thought, instantly tuning out all conversation and getting prickly all over.

Get hold of yourself, I warned. You've thought
that before. There are thousands of green cars
with dents in their rear right fenders.

But the feeling wouldn't go away. Suddenly it
was as if I was in a capsule, all by myself, closed
off from everyone.

"Hey, why so quiet?" Kim asked, poking my
arm playfully.

"She's probably thinking of David," Sue answered for me.

"I think I saw his car."

They both looked at each other, then at me.
"Where?"

"It's gone already."

"Maybe we should call the police. . . ."

"Andrea . . . are you *sure*?" Sue asked.

"I don't know. I thought it was." I said no more. More than once fear had colored my vision. Sue's challenge made me doubt. Pull yourself together, I demanded of myself again. Come on now. *You're over that.* Start walking, and forget it. You were probably wrong.

"No. I guess not. Let's go," I said.

All through lunch they tried to get me to talk about it, but I wouldn't. While one part of me chatted about clothes and movies, another part was busy comparing what I'd seen with what I remembered, and the two images did seem frighteningly identical. Maybe I should have called Corbett, I thought one second. The next I'd think, it wasn't him. You'd just make a lot of trouble. By the time we left the falafel place, I'd almost persuaded myself that of course I'd been wrong.

We were almost at the art store. Sue was talking, when I chanced to look straight ahead, and there he was . . . coming toward me.

Every time I'd ever imagined how it would be, I saw this heroic image of myself. I'd go running at him, scratch his eyes, scream for help, kick him, punch him, but not, under any circumstances, let him pass.

But it wasn't that way at all. All I did was stand still and cover my face and start to scream inside all over again. And then my legs folded.

When I came to, I was on the ground and my head was cradled in Sue's lap. She was stroking my hair and her face, bent over mine, looked white and anxious. She kept saying, "Andrea! Andrea!"

I curled up into a ball to make myself as small a target as possible and answered with a terrible wailing scream that wouldn't stop and couldn't possibly be coming from me.

When I finally quieted down, I realized there was a crowd watching, and hid my face, ashamed. Kim and Sue helped me up and pushed through the crowd, keeping their arms around me until we reached the car. There I told them what happened. Kim rushed off to phone Corbett. But by the time the police came, *he* might well have been in Mexico.

We drove home then, not talking much. I sat stunned, having these little shivering fits. My teeth would begin to chatter as if I was freezing. While Sue drove, Kim rubbed my icy hands and cuddled me whenever the shaking got too bad.

But finally I began to feel better. As we neared home, I started thinking of Mom's reaction. In Newport she'd been almost impatient with my "imagined" fears. I'd stopped telling her about how I felt in school, as much to spare me as her. And though she'd once said that maybe I needed help, I honestly believed she'd rather sweep everything that happened under the rug. To present her with this newest sign of my "psychotic" behavior would only throw her back to the beginning. She'd have to face up to her own fears all over again and face the fact that you don't get over rape like you do the flu.

"Please don't tell Mom," I told Sue. "I was just

overreacting. She'll think I'm ready for the loony bin."

"Uh-uh!" She replied, darting me a determined look. "No more pussyfooting around to spare her! You need help, Andrea. You really do! I could kick myself for being so unfeeling before. Gee, Andy. I just didn't realize." She took a hand off the wheel to touch mine and gave me the most caring, gentle smile I'd ever seen.

"You *have* to see someone!" Kim picked up. "A professional, Andrea! It's long overdue. We'll talk to your mother, and your dad, too. They have to get help."

"It's so expensive . . ."

"Spensive-shmensive!" Sue said. "I've got savings!"

I started to cry then, and I don't think I stopped till we got home.

Two days later, I started therapy.

Before, I said sometimes things get worse before they can get better. Well, going into therapy was when the change for the better began.

I started going to Rae every day for an hour. She saw Mom and Dad, too, but not as often. It wasn't at all like I expected. I thought psychologists were gray-haired and owlish-looking, and you had to lie down on a couch while he or she sat in a chair behind you taking notes.

Rae's office was a small guesthouse in back of her home. It had a slightly musty odor from the pool nearby, but it was bright and cheerful because of the big picture window looking out onto the lawn. I'd sit in a leather chair opposite the couch, and Rae—a little woman with dark curly hair and half-glasses—would usually hand me a can of iced tea from the small refrigerator nearby, and then we'd just talk. Sometimes she'd take notes, but mostly she'd just listen, ask me a question now and then, and maybe pick up a blanket she was knitting for her grandchild and work on it, watching me over the half-glasses while her hands worked automatically.

Mostly we talked about feelings, like guilt and anger. "Every time I think of it," I said one day, "I'm sure I should have fought back with every ounce of strength, kicked him, poked his eyes out!"

"Rapists *can* sometimes be scared off if a victim resists," Rae said, needles clicking away rapidly. "But that man held a gun to your head. He weighed a hundred and seventy pounds. You weigh a hundred and eighteen. You followed your instincts, Andrea, which were to survive. If you'd resisted too much, he might have killed you. Think about that." She gathered up some more pink yarn and wrapped it around a finger.

I did think about it, and felt better. But the guilt was more complex than just that. It was that there had to be a reason for it all to make sense, and there didn't seem to be one, unless I could blame myself. Had I worn something too provocative?

Looked at him in a way I hadn't intended? Was God punishing me for disobeying my mother?

"There's a rape every nine minutes in the United States," Rae said. "Nearly every victim asks herself those same questions, but the truth is, rape is not a crime of passion. It's a crime of *rage*."

One day I cried, "I'm so sick of pretending everything's fine! I get so angry, having to fake what I feel!"

"Yes, yes, get angry! That's good! Come on, punch something! Pretend it's him! Scream! Let that anger out! It will help you heal," she said.

We talked about lots of things, during those hours of therapy—guilt and hate, shame and fear, and even my longing to be as I had once been—able to sit on a bus again, to walk down the street again . . . innocent, trusting, fearless.

But Rae couldn't give me that. She said I couldn't change what happened, only learn to live with it. She said that what happened would leave a scar, that I'd never be quite the same carefree person I once was. But that being cautious wasn't so terrible, was it, within bounds?

Seeing Rae, having someone to put my feelings into perspective, someone who wasn't emotionally connected to me, did help. And in the later visits, we even talked of what would happen if they caught him.

"When the police find him, your anger will give you the courage to stand up to him in court. And once he's convicted, much of your fear will disappear," Rae said.

"Do you really think they'll find him?"

"It's possible."

"And do you really want me to go through all that again in court?"

"It's not what I want, but what you want." Rae challenged me over her glasses, then lowered her eyes to pick up a stitch. "But I'll tell you this. When the time comes to make that decision, I think you'll know what to do."

She was right. I'd asked the question automatically, and I think that even then I had decided.

Three weeks before Christmas I got a call from Corbett. "We're going to conduct a lineup," he said. "We'd like you to come to the station and view some individuals."

My heart jumped and I nearly dropped the phone. "Did you *find* him?"

"I didn't say it was him."

"But you wouldn't ask me if you didn't think it was!"

"Don't jump to conclusions, Andrea," Corbett said. "When can you come down?"

My mother clutched her throat when she heard the news. Then she said, "Thank God. Every time you left the house, I've worried."

Sue said, "If it is . . . will you press charges?"

I looked at Mother and answered *her*. "Yes."

"Good," Sue said. "You've really got guts."

"Andrea . . ." Mother started to say.

"No, Mom. Don't let's argue that. Even if there's only a one percent chance he'll go to jail, I've *got* to."

Daddy drove me to the station. I was so uptight, I could hardly breathe. Dad didn't say a word the whole way. Before we got out, it struck me that he must feel pretty shaky, too. I put a hand on his arm and said, "Daddy dear. Please. If it *is* him, let the police handle it from here. Promise you won't do anything. He's sick, Daddy. He needs help."

Daddy nodded and kissed me on the forehead. "The chick teaching the rooster," he said.

Corbett couldn't give us any details. He said that *if* it was the man, and *if* I decided to prosecute, and *if* he was convicted, *then* he could tell me the circumstances under which he had been arrested. But until then, he couldn't prejudice me one way or the other with such facts.

"You'll be behind a glass," he explained. "Only one side, your side, can see through. On the other side of the glass you'll see six men lined up. I'll give you a sheet of paper. You'll mark on it which, if any, is the man." Corbett stood up. "Andrea? You ready? Think you can handle it?"

My icy hands were clasped tightly against my lips. Daddy pried them free and held them in his. I got up; Daddy did, too. My legs had the shakes, and I had to hold onto the desk for a minute.

"I'm sorry, Mr. Cranston," Corbett said, "but I'd rather you didn't come with Andrea." I guess

Corbett thought Daddy might get violent. Surprisingly Dad didn't object, thanks to Rae's talks,
maybe. All he did was squeeze my arm encour-
agingly and kiss my forehead when I turned a
scared smile on him. Then I marched off down the
hall with Corbett.

In my mind's eye, his face came alive again,
emblazoned across my brain cells in neon lights.
In a second I might really be looking at him. Even
though he couldn't see me, I would feel he could.
How would I react? Would I embarrass myself
and throw up? Would all that happened that day
come back?

Corbett opened a door to a small room. One
wall of it was all glass. He offered me a chair and
I sat in it, leaning forward, hands tightly clasped.
The room behind the glass was lit, but empty.
Corbett spoke into a microphone. "All right, you
can bring them in now."

Six men filed into the room and stood against
the wall, blinking at the bright light. I shut my
eyes tight, then opened them. The men looked
somewhat alike. But I knew instantly. Even
though his hair was grown in, it was *him*.

"I want each of you to step forward, one at a
time. When you reach the white line, you will give
us a right profile, then a left profile. Then you will
face forward and say, 'Just do as I say, and I won't
hurt you.'" Corbett said.

I sat in the chair, as cold as an ice cube, bent
forward, peering at him through the glass. *It
just didn't seem possible he couldn't see me.* The

invisible chain that I've always felt connected us seemed to lead from me straight through the glass to him.

One by one the men did as Corbett ordered. But it was number four whose number I wrote in giant print on my paper even before the first man stepped out. I was shivering now, and Corbett came up and put a hand on my shoulder. He looked down at my number and switched the mike off. He asked, "Why do you think it's him?"

"The eyes . . . those green, arrogant eyes. It's the mole near the ear. It's—everything. It's *him!*" I whispered.

Number three stepped forward, and then, finally, number four—*him.* I held my breath, waiting to hear him speak, and not wanting to hear his voice.

"Just do as I say, and I won't hurt you," he said, looking straight at me. There was no anger, no hate, no viciousness in the tone. Just expressionless words. But it was *his* voice. I'd know it without seeing his face. And it all started to come back.

I buried my face in my hands and started to cry, because I just couldn't stand any more.

The wheels of justice grind slowly, they say. It must be true because it's five months since the lineup. Tomorrow, at last, we go to trial.

I'm so scared! I felt safe these last months because he was in jail. But tomorrow decides if he stays there. And what if he doesn't?

Corbett said they caught him in the hills near Brentwood. There was a girl in his car, raped, beaten, and tied up on the floor in the front. When he stopped for gas she managed to hit the gas pedal, making the car spurt forward. It hit a gas pump. The man just sped off before anyone could stop him, but an attendant got his license number and phoned the police.

So there are two of us bringing charges.

This morning I woke early and put on the clothes I had selected so carefully last night. From the bathroom came the buzz of Dad's electric razor; from the kitchen the smell of coffee brewing. Jeff would be setting the breakfast table, I figured, because when he did it, you could hear silver clattering and cups knocking against each other.

I sat on the edge of my bed, hands clasped in my lap, waiting, thinking, trying not to feel.

David called last night. We'd seen a lot of each other over Christmas and written since, but this was the first time he'd ever phoned. "Just wanted you to know I'll be with you, Andy," he said. His voice was like a touch, soft and gentle. I nodded at the phone and wiped a tear from my cheek.

"Scared?"

"Terrified."

"I know. . . ."

And I knew he did. I knew he, too, pictured what it would be like, a courtroom full of strangers watching me tell all those personal things—and him—in the witness chair, facing me . . .

I shook my head, wanting to clear it of thoughts like that, when Mom knocked at the door and came in.

Her eyes went to my face, not to what I was wearing, and she smiled. "Breakfast is ready, honey." She held her arms out to me as she came forward. "Sure you don't want me there, too?"

"Oh, Mom!" I leaped from the bed to her arms, hugging her tight and shivering against her chest. Six months ago she could have never offered that!

An hour or so later I entered the courtroom, walking between Luisa from the Rape Hotline, and Sue. Yes, Sue! How strange and wonderful that she had wanted to come, that despite all the bitterness between us earlier, I wanted her there!

As for Mom and Dad, that was a different thing. I couldn't bear to see their faces if I was asked to describe in any detail what he had done. But they were with me in spirit; I knew that now.

It was a closed trial. That means outsiders couldn't just wander in off the streets. Such a relief! For weeks I'd worried that half the school would be there, cutting classes just so they could watch and listen.

District Attorney Madison (representing me) was flipping through some papers when we came in and sat down. He looked up and smiled at me, then sauntered over and hunched down on his heels to talk. "They'll be bringing him in in a minute, Andrea. I'm going to put you on first. Ginny will testify after you." He nodded toward a dark-haired girl sitting behind me. An older woman sat beside her. "Now, listen," he said, his eyes returning to me. "Don't let him get to you. Just stay cool and answer my questions just the way you did in my office."

"But what about his law—the public defender?" The words stuck in my throat, and I didn't finish. Every time I'd seen Madison I'd asked the same question. It was the public defender who could make me look bad. He could twist my words, infer things that weren't so. He could make *me* look guilty. It happened. I'd seen it on TV.

"Just answer his questions like you do mine. The truth can't hurt you."

Luisa and Sue kept up a steady stream of small talk to keep my mind off what lay ahead. But only a small part of me listened. The rest concentrated on that side door through which he'd be coming.

When they brought him in, his pale eyes slid around the room, taking in the jury, the judge, the few people seated, and me. He smiled—as if we were dear friends. *Smiled!* My heart stopped. Why would he do that? What would the jury think?

I was called to the stand right after the introductory remarks. My mouth went dry and my legs became wet spaghetti. Sue squeezed my arm and Luisa whispered, "You'll be fine!"

I had to pass his row. For an awful second I

thought he'd reach out and grab me, kill me, something! I almost ran the few steps to the witness stand. There Madison took my arm and led me to the chair. When I was seated and sworn in I looked first at the jury with all their eyes fixed so solemnly on me. Then at him.

He was still smiling.

Madison must have sensed how close to blacking out I was, because very casually he positioned himself so that he blocked my line of view. "Now Andrea," he said quietly, "will you tell the jury just what happened."

Step by step, question by question, he drew my story out. My body wasn't being violated. My life wasn't being threatened. Yet I was being drawn again into the events of that day, forced to tell those unknown people watching me how it was. I was too scared, too involved in my own emotions to wonder if they believed me, to examine their eyes for signs of doubt, contempt, understanding, or whatever. It was as if my body was on an operating table being dissected while an audience of student doctors looked on, but the real me was elsewhere, observing it all.

Then the public defender stepped forward. I drew myself together and took a deep breath waiting for the blow. But it never came! Not once did he question me about the rape. The only thing he wanted to know was this: "Are you absolutely certain that this man, here, is the one?"

"Yes!" I said, meeting his eyes without flinching. "Yes. He has a mole behind his ear. He has a gold tooth on the bottom left. His hair is longer now, but yes, He is the one!"

It's over at last. He was convicted on several counts—rape, child molesting, assault and battery, other things. He'll get five years to life!

I feel so good! He's locked away. I feel so—free! The chain that linked me to him all this time is cut at last, though I suspect I'll always drag an end.

Rae says that's how it is, that what happened leaves a scar. "If you pick at it," she warns, "it begins to ooze again. So mostly, you just leave it alone. Let it heal. And it will, slowly. . . ."